A Tale Of Two

Ninja Kids

Book 6

The Battle For The Shinwa Forest

By Adam Oakley

COPYRIGHT

ISBN: 978-1-912720-64-4

www.NinjaKidsBook.com

www.InnerPeaceNow.com

www.AdamOakleyBooks.com

Published by Oakhouse Publications.

Oakhouse Publications

Contents

歓
迎

Welcome

Nunchuks

Throwing Darts

Throwing Stars

Daggers

Young Warrior

Ninja Swords

Chapter 1 - Success

When Martin returned from his time-travelling mission, now wearing two coats that had fused into one, he wasn't sure if his mission to put a stop to the creation of destructive Treemakers had been a success. After freeing his mother, Amanda, from the prison of her own memories, they had met with the Garganfan in the forest and decided to see if they could find Ellogog, the first tree created by Jacobson Muldridge's Treemaker.

Ellogog the tree had not moved since he laid down his roots to rest by the Healing Lake. Martin was confused.

"So Ellogog is here, that must mean Treemakers still exist. He was planted by a Treemaker," Martin said.

"No," Martin's mother said. "No. He wasn't."

"He was, Mum, we came here together, he said he wanted a rest. Ellogog, Ellogog can you hear me?"

"Its name is Ellogog," his mother said. "But he says he wasn't born from a Treemaker."

"How can you tell?" Martin said.

"I'm a Tree Whisperer too. And I've learnt by now that I simply have to listen."

Martin realised he was not listening to the tree at all. He was just placing his ideas onto it.

"That was one of my gifts," Amanda said, taking a deep breath in. "I could communicate with plant life very easily."

Martin looked at the Garganfan.

"Any other ideas?" Martin said. "Ellogog, will you come to life like you did before? Can you get up and move around?"

Martin listened for an answer this time. He heard Ellogog's voice speak back to him:

"I am perfectly happy here. I have no need to move."

Martin paused for a moment. His mother had her eyes closed.

"So...do you even remember the Treemaker, the whole thing with the other trees who wanted to take revenge on the humans?"

"Yes," Ellogog said. "But that is now in another version of time. It seems you changed things."

"How did you get here then?" Martin said. "If I changed things, how did you get to be beside this lake?"

"I don't know. My memory of my birth is hazy. I think it may have something to do with that coat you're wearing."

Martin realised that he had not seen Geraldo in a while. He wondered if he would even accompany him into the present, when he was no longer travelling through time.

"Yes," Geraldo said, sitting above Martin in the branches of a tree. "I am always with you when you are wearing at least one coat. But you don't always need my advice. Sometimes you don't even want it."

"Well I do now," Martin said. "How has this happened, Geraldo? How is Ellogog here if I succeeded in helping Rayner escape with his family, so that he didn't feel the need to take his revenge on humans?"

"Your desire placed Ellogog here. You wanted him to be here, and with the power of those two coats you are wearing, your intention alone was enough."

"So I can control things?" Martin said.

"In a way, yes," Geraldo said. "Everyone can, but with those two coats merged into one, your signals into the universe become amplified. They become clearer, less muddled like most people's."

Martin let out a sigh of relief.

"So I did it? I stopped Rayner from building all those destructive Treemakers?"

"Yes."

"And where is he now?"

"In another world."

Martin sat down. The Garganfan and his mother did the same.

"So...so what is left now?" Martin said. "Is there anything else I need to do?"

"There's just one thing," Geraldo said.

"What?" Martin said.

"It's to do with the whereabouts of the third and final coat..."

Success

Success is primarily a state of being.

Chapter 2 - The Third And Final Coat

"I remember you now," Amanda said as she, Martin, the Garganfan and Geraldo were walking through the woods towards Jacobson Muldridge's house.

"Yes. We have met, haven't we?" the Garganfan said. "When you were much younger."

"You taught us how to fight," Amanda said. "My body feels completely different now. It's as if all those powers and skills I developed are flooding back into me." Martin watched his mother utter a few words to a tree beside her, the tree seemed to move slightly as if it was nodding, and then she jumped, climbed and began to scamper up into the upper branches of the tree.

Martin couldn't believe it.

"She's completely different," Martin said. "She even looks different."

"And she will continue to change," the Garganfan said. "She has re-discovered her power."

"Can they see you?" Martin said to Geraldo. Geraldo shook his head.

"No, but they can sense I am here. They have already heard you speaking to me."

"There's a guide with me," Martin said, as his mother clambered quickly back down the tree as if she was a strong, agile child.

"Yes, I thought so," she said. "What's its name?"

"Geraldo. He's been helping me as I've gone through time. As long as I wear these coats, I can see him."

"The coat is a different colour now," the Garganfan said.

"Yes," Martin said, "I'm wearing two. They have merged together, and Geraldo says I have to do something with the third one. Do I have to find it, Geraldo?"

"Yes. You have to steal it," Geraldo said.

"Really?" Martin said. "But..."

"I know, I know," Geraldo said. "Stealing is wrong, I know. But in this case, it is necessary. The coat is in some dangerous hands. If they work out what it can actually be used for, there will be dangers for the rest of you."

"Well where is it?" Martin said.

"Over there," Geraldo nodded.

Martin, the Garganfan and Amanda looked over to Jacobson Muldridge's house.

7

"Really?" Martin said. "But Jacobson was demonstralised by Nerris, he doesn't have any truly bad intentions..."

"He was demonstralised," Geraldo said, "but the effects are not permanent. You surely saw him re-growing some kind of tyrannical tendencies when he had hold of his own Treemaker. Although the Treemakers no longer exist due to the changes you made in your timeline, the tyrannical tendency is still growing within him, and his coat is somewhere in that house."

"Whereabouts?"

"In a dark room upstairs, in the far right corner of the house, beneath a picture of Jacobson's father."

*

Jacobson Muldridge was eating lunch with his son, Arthur.

"Arthur. Arthur please keep your mouth closed when you are chewing."

Arthur shut his mouth. Both of them had calmer energies now. Jacobson was still feeling the effects of being demonstralised, and Arthur had been humbled by his experience of being dragged away into the forest by a Bodysnatcher, only to soon be saved by the Garganfan.

A servant of Jacobson's walked in. She was holding a bowlful of peas.

"The peas are late!" Jacobson snapped. He shocked himself. It was as if something very dark, something very cold and deep within him was reaching up to grab at his mind.

His flash of anger passed.

"Sorry, I'm sorry, my dear. Thank you. Thank you for the peas."

"You're welcome, sir. Sorry they are so late."

As Jacobson watched the peas being served onto his plate, he began to feel a heat burning inside of him. He couldn't control it.

"Not too many!" he said. "I don't like too many."

"Sorry, sir," the servant said. "Shall I remove some?"

"Yes. Don't remove too many!" he shouted.

As the servant removed one too many peas from Jacobson's plate, Jacobson stood, overcome by a saturation of fury that swept up from within him, and he pushed the servant so hard that she tripped, fell and the hot peas landed all over her.

Another servant walked in. A young man named Gregor.

"Elizabeth!" Gregor yelled, and as he ran over to help her, Jacobson stood there, stunned, wondering what he had just done.

"Elizabeth," Jacobson said, "Elizabeth I'm so sorry, I don't know what came over..."

"Leave her alone, sir!" Gregor said, still managing to keep his respectful tone.

Elizabeth had burns on her neck.

"Elizabeth," Jacobson said again, "I'm so sorry. Take her to the medical room, Gregor, please, I..."

Gregor didn't know whether to lash out at Jacobson, or keep himself safe and just take Elizabeth away. He helped Elizabeth to her feet, and he led her away to the medical room.

*

"He shouldn't have done that, that was abuse," Gregor said in their living quarters that evening. Many of Jacobson's staff lived on the property, in the same home, in a very tidy but small section of the house where they each had a bedroom and a main living room to share. Elizabeth had bandaging around her neck from the burns. She was sitting opposite Gregor.

"Don't worry," Elizabeth said. "Don't get yourself worked up, Gregor."

"I can't help it. I thought he'd changed. I thought he was different. The boy, too. But no, that man's just as nasty as ever. He had never laid a finger on any of us before! It's as if something dark in him, the worst part has been hidden for a while, and now it's coming back to the surface."

"Well what can we do?" Elizabeth said. "Report him?"

"That won't work. He's too friendly with the chief of police. He's done worse things to people who don't work for him, and the reports seem to fall on deaf ears."

"Maybe we should forgive him," Elizabeth said. "Maybe he really has changed."

"Don't," Gregor said. "Just don't, Elizabeth. You make far too many allowances for his bad behaviour. You always have."

"But we still have two years left on those contracts we signed," Elizabeth said. "When he told us it was job security all those years ago, I didn't realise..."

"There must be something," Gregor said. "There must be something we can use for bargaining power. Right now it says that if we work elsewhere, he will be entitled to eighty percent of our salaries. It even says that the contracts can not be changed, even by himself in the future. It's almost as if he knew that one day he might temporarily lighten up for a while..."

"Well what then?" Elizabeth said. "What can we do?"

"I don't know," Gregor said. "He keeps everything valuable locked away, doesn't he?"

"Hmm," Elizabeth said, looking at the ground.

"What?"

"There is one thing. I like it. It's probably nothing..."

"No, go on, what is it?" Gregor said.

"It's probably not even valuable. But it certainly looks it. I don't think he's ever even worn it..."

"Well what is it?"

"You know the room he has in honour of his father? The one that we are told is out of bounds? That big old room in the corner of the house?"

Gregor nodded.

"Well, in that room there's the most beautiful coat I've ever seen. I saw it once when the door was open for a moment. It's big, long and silvery and luxurious. It's on display. I overheard him say once that his father had promised him to never keep it locked away. Apparently his father had tried to lock it up once to keep it safe, and the coat destroyed the entire building."

Gregor snorted with a laugh.

"A coat? A coat destroyed a building. How? Set fire to it?" Gregor snorted again.

"That's what I've heard him saying to Arthur," Elizabeth said. "Arthur wanted to put it on, but Jacobson also said that his father had made him promise to never wear it or let anyone else wear it."

"Well," Gregor said, dismissing the mystery around the coat but recognising its value in Jacobson's mind. "Well, then, let's say this. Why don't we go up there, tonight, and take it for ourselves?"

"No," Elizabeth said. "No that would be far too dangerous for us. Imagine what he'd do."

"We'd demand to leave, or else we'd destroy the coat. Cut it in half. With scissors. And he must *pay us* to leave. A donation, not a salary. Enough money so that we can live the rest of our lives in peace, and we don't have to keep getting jobs that we don't like."

"I don't know," Elizabeth said. "It sounds too risky."

"You know how friendly I am with the security team."

"Not all of them," Elizabeth said. "Some of them don't like you at all. It's too dangerous, Gregor."

Gregor stared at her.

"Okay," he said. "You don't have to join me. But I'm going to get that coat. Tonight."

Determination

A determined mind does not fight obstacles,
but finds the swiftest way around them.

Chapter 3 - A Thief In The Night

It was getting dark in the forest beyond the Muldridge residence. Martin, Amanda, the Garganfan and Geraldo were sitting, staring at the huge house across the expanse of land ahead of them.

"It's getting dark quickly," Martin said. "Why is that?"

"It's your coats," Geraldo said. "They accelerate time when they are in full harmony."

"Why?"

"They carry such a high vibrational frequency that they speed up everything around you. Their resting power speeds the passing of time.

"It's best to wait until dark, anyway," Geraldo continued. "You began your training as a ninja, and now you must honour it by sneaking into that house and retrieving the final coat."

"What do you think Jacobson will do?" Martin said.

"I'm not sure he's actually the one to worry about," Geraldo said. "It might be someone else."

"Alright then, I'll just pop in there and pop back out," Martin said. "I can do anything with these coats I'm wearing, you've already shown me that."

"Not in your original timeline," Geraldo said. "Their active powers are only accessible once you are actually time travelling. When you wear them in your own time frame, all they do is speed up time."

Soon it was completely dark around them.

"So I've really got no powers now?" Martin said. He had his heart set on popping in and out of Jacobson's house, just through thought. "Why am I even wearing the other two coats then? I should take them off and slow things down..."

Martin started to reach to his sleeves and pull off the two coats that had now become one.

"Wait," the Garganfan said, staring at Martin in the dark. "The story of the three coats is that the third is the most cunning and elusive. While the first two enjoy serving a higher purpose, ideally uniting for a common cause, the third coat does not want to be found or used for good. It's known as the vengeful coat, the coat that resented being created, sentenced to having to live for an eternity, only to be used as a tool by whoever would wear it. So the coat rebels. It seeks to cause harm, for harm's sake. It needs no higher motive, as Rayner did. Rayner wanted revenge, but he also wanted to bring peace to the world of trees."

Martin thought for a moment. His question had not been answered.

"But why do I have to wear the coats?"

"The story says that the vengeful coat can only be tamed by the wearer of the other two. It has a certain loyalty to its kin. You will be safer wearing the coats that it was born alongside."

Martin paused again. He could almost feel the two coats pulsing a dormant power through his bones and out into the world around him.

"Why didn't Rayner ever wear two coats at once?" Martin said, looking at the glint of blue on his sleeves.

"Perhaps he didn't think of it," Geraldo said. "Or perhaps they refused to merge with him as the wearer. Luckily with your pure intentions, the coats were happy to work together after a short period of time."

Martin took a deep breath in, and let a long breath out.

"You are forgetting all of the powers you have already developed, first with Kuyasaki and now with the Garganfan," Geraldo said. "You cannot rely on the coats now. You have to use the powers within you."

"Okay," Martin said. "So what do I do, go in there, get the coat, and get out of there again?"

"Yes," Geraldo said. "But don't put the coat on. Its vengeful intentions can take over even the purest of minds. If there is even a trace of darkness within you, it will latch on to it, feed it and empower it so that you become the slave of the coat, and not the other way around. It likes to use people, not serve them."

"Right," Martin said. "Well here I go."

"Good luck," the Garganfan said.

"You can do it, Martin," Amanda said, confidently. He looked at her for a moment, and in the darkness he felt as if she wasn't quite the same mother anymore. Their relationship had changed. They were becoming completely independent.

"Don't I need help?" Martin said, delaying his departure. He didn't want to drag his mother into this, but the Garganfan was good at fighting.

"Garganfans are clumsy when cut off from nature," the Garganfan said. "In an enclosed space I would be unnecessarily noisy, and stealth is the aim here."

"I will stay with you," Geraldo said.

Martin looked up at the house, who's indoor lights were gradually being switched off as the entire household went to sleep. Martin took one more deep breath, and launched himself across the darkness of the land.

Speed

Speed is built through consistent repetition.

Chapter 4 - The Retrieval

As soon as Martin began sprinting across the darkness of Jacobson's land towards his house, the floodlights snapped on. The entire field was illuminated. After Myasako had broken in to save Amanda, Jacobson had ordered security to tighten up, and had employed more guards.

The floodlights were so bright that it made Martin squint, but soon he had dived into a row of hedges, and he was waiting for something.

He didn't know what he was waiting for. His instincts had taken over. Time seemed to be passing quickly, and yet it was as if everything was moving in slow motion. He didn't know if it was because of the coats he was wearing or the skills he had developed during his time with Kuyasaki and then the Garganfan, but his mind was in a completely different state to normal. It was as if he was connected to the whole universe.

"It ran in there!" he heard a gruff voice say. Footsteps were approaching, running footsteps that made Martin feel as if he was sinking into the soil beneath him.

"Don't move," he heard another voice say. It sounded like the hedge beside him had just whispered in his ear.

Martin obeyed. He didn't move.

"Alright," the gruff voice said. "We've seen you're in there! Now come out!"

Martin could see through the thicket of hedges that there were three large guards. They were holding weapons that Martin couldn't quite see.

"What was it?" one of them said. "Was it a person? Looked more like a fox."

"It wasn't a fox! It was running on two legs."

"Looked low to the ground to me. Could've been a..."

"It was a person!" the main guard said. "I saw him run right in here."

Martin held his breath.

"Shoot. Shoot at it."

"No way," one of the guards said. "You know what the boss is like about plants these days. He said that if anyone cuts down anything without his permission, he'll have them fired. He was talking about plants like they're people. He's turned weird. One moment he's all loving and kind, the next he seems to be like his old self, I wonder if..."

"Concentrate!" the main guard hissed. "Fine. Go in there then. Go and take a look."

Martin felt a bright flashlight shine onto his face. He closed his eyes.

"No, I'm not going in there," the other guard said. "Foxes can be vicious."

"Me neither," another one said.

The main guard let out a sigh of frustration.

"Fine!" he said. The guard took a deep breath in for courage, and then dived into the row of hedges with a knife brandished in one hand, and a firearm in the other.

He was jamming his knife into all the gaps he could see. Martin opened his eyes slightly. "Stay there," he heard the hedge say again. The knife shot past his face, past his arm, over his leg and then stopped a few inches from his stomach.

The guard clambered out again.

"All I see is hedges," the guard said. "It's just hedges."

"Told you it was a fox," one of the guards said.

There was a moment of silence.

"Right, all of us, now, just have a look in the rest of this hedgerow. Perhaps you were right. But I was sure..."

"Who do you know that can run that fast, and that low to the ground?" the second guard said. "It was definitely an animal."

"Hmm," the main guard said. "It *was* moving fast. Alright. Check the rest of the hedge and then get back to main posts."

"Alright," the second guard said

"Yes, sir," the third guard said.

Martin watched them check the rest of the hedgerow, before they finally walked off.

"Thanks," Martin said to the hedge.

"You are one of us," the hedge replied. "Now go!"

Martin quickly leapt out of the bushes and ran around the side of the house. He found a glass door. He reached out and touched the handle. It was unlocked. He looked into the house through the door, saw no one, and opened it.

Geraldo flew into the house as Martin ran in.

Martin saw his own reflection in a mirror.

"Is that me?" He stopped and stared. He almost looked like a man. He was much taller, much more muscular than he had ever remembered seeing himself.

"Don't get distracted," Geraldo said. "The room is at the far right corner of the house."

"Okay," Martin said. "Show me the way."

Geraldo trotted off down the corridor and looked around the corner.

"It's clear," Geraldo said. "Now come on!"

*

"I'm going, I'm going right now," Gregor said.

"Don't," Elizabeth said. "Please, Gregor, just don't."

"He has to pay for what he did to you. Those burns might leave scars," Gregor said.

The two servants, Elizabeth and Gregor, were standing alone together in the shared living room. They should have been in bed at this time. Past eleven o'clock, if you weren't working, you were not allowed outside of your room.

"Listen," Gregor said. He trotted up to the closed door that led into the main part of the house and he heard two guards talking as they walked past.

"Definitely just a fox," one of them said. "No way could that have been a person."

"Yeh," the other guard said. "I like foxes."

The two of them continued to repeat themselves all the way down the corridor outside the servants' living quarters, until their voices disappeared.

"Those two are going to bed. They are making the switch for the night shifts," Gregor said. "Goodbye, Elizabeth."

Before Elizabeth could say anything else or grab him and try to hold him in the safety of the living room, Gregor had opened the door into the main house, and he was gone.

*

Martin still had the strange feeling that time was passing quickly, but he could see everything in slow motion. Most of the house was dark, apart from the moonlight that would shine in and light up some of the rooms just enough for Martin to see the obstacles around him.

The house was full of small tables and large paintings on the walls that sometimes Martin would glue himself to if he thought anyone was coming. Then he heard some voices. It was two of the guards from earlier.

"He should leave more lights on," one of them said. "I can hardly see a thing!"

"He said it's a waste," the other one said.

27

"I know! I know he did," the first one said, "but it's no good for us, is it? It's no good for security. I remember a time where the lights never went off, he didn't give a damn about the environment, he said he..."

"What was that?"

"Dunno."

"Did you hear it?"

"Yeh."

"It sounded like running."

"Yeh."

"Come on. Get the lights on. No one should be running through the house, especially at this time!"

Martin listened to the two guards shuffle off away from him in the direction of the running noise that they could hear.

He followed them. Ahead of him he could see the two bumbling guards turning corners and hitting any light switches they could to help them do their job.

"What are they chasing?" Martin asked.

"I think someone else is on the same mission as you, but for a different reason," Geraldo said.

Martin kept following the sounds and occasional sights of the two guards as they ran through ornate corridors and made it to the foot of a spiral staircase.

Martin could hear them hissing at each other.

"Where are we going now? I can't hear it anymore," one of them said.

The guards stopped running. They were both out of breath. Martin peered around the corner at them.

"I dunno. I was sure I heard it. Sounded like someone ran into a table too, didn't it?"

"Yeh."

"We're supposed to be off duty now, he has us working too hard. The other guards are getting paid to do nothing! Let's just go back to the living quarters."

"Yeh."

The guards turned back and now began walking in Martin's direction.

Martin looked behind him and saw that there were two new guards turning the corner and beginning to walk towards him too. Perhaps the guards were about to trade places for the evening.

Martin had nowhere to go. He was about to be seen.

"What do I do now?" he thought, staring at Geraldo.

"Why did you follow those guards in the first place?" Geraldo said.

"I don't know," Martin quickly thought, "I suppose I got distracted."

"It was reckless," Geraldo said. "They led you away from where you wanted to be. Distractions can pretend to be tempting, but they do you little good at all. Now you'll have to pay the price."

"Help me," Martin said. "I don't want to have to fight."

"Then don't. Don't fight," Geraldo said.

"Oi!" Martin heard one of the previously running guards shout. Martin's back was up against the wall, but he was sure he was visible to them.

"Oi what are you two doing here! You're supposed to wait for us in the living quarters!"

Martin's eyes shifted right and saw the two new guards walking down the corridor towards him.

"You're late," one of the new guards said. The tone of his voice already sounded far more intelligent than the other two guards. It sounded clear, well-mannered but cutting.

"We thought we heard something. Running."

"And what did you find?" the same new guard said.

"Nothin'. Nothin'."

The two pairs of guards met in front of Martin. He wasn't sure how he hadn't been seen. He was pressed up so tightly against the wooden wall behind him, and he hadn't noticed the leaves of the large house plant that he was standing beside were touching his sleeves.

"Why can't they see me?" Martin thought. Geraldo was standing opposite him on the other side of the corridor. Martin saw Geraldo nod to the large plant beside Martin.

"Hello," Martin thought.

"Hello," the plant whispered back. "I'm helping. You are one of us. We have all been told to help you."

Martin took a moment to fully realise that every plant he was now encountering seemed willing to help him, and seemed willing to somehow present him to the world as one of them, a plant in the eyes of other human beings. First the hedge outside had helped him, and now this house plant was helping him too.

"Don't move though," the plant said. "If they see you move, it will be like watching a plant walking across the floor. They won't like it."

"Okay," Martin thought.

"And make sure you keep contact with me," the plant said. "I can only help you if we are touching."

"Okay," Martin thought. "Thanks."

He listened to the guards speak. The conversation was not long. The two new guards clearly held a disdain for the slow-wittedness of the other two. Martin found the two new guards to be far more menacing. At one point, one of them turned his head towards Martin and stared at him in the eyes.

"Since when were there two plants there?" the guard said.

Martin had already noticed the weapons at the waists of all four guards.

"Dunno," one of the others said. "Don't matter, does it? Just a plant."

"Hmm," the noticing guard said. "Just odd, that's all. Very well. Now get to bed, you two. We are taking over the corridor patrol. Goodnight."

"Night," the first guard said

"Night," the other one said, and the two pairs of guards walked down the corridor, away from each other.

"Will you let me lead you now?" Geraldo said. "You just have to trust me."

"Lead the way," Martin said. "No more distractions. I just wanted to see if someone else really had broken in..."

"You will see soon enough," Geraldo said. "Now let's go."

See

To see clearly, do not use the eyes of the past.

Chapter 5 - Stealth

Gregor had very little stealth. He was filled with panic and excitement and fear and dread and regret and all sorts of emotions that meant his footsteps were heavy and his passage was clumsy as he scrambled down corridors and up stairs, luckily avoiding the guards at all levels of the house until he reached the top floor.

He was bounding up some stairs, as quietly as he could but still making shuffling and clicking noises as he stepped.

He looked around a corner and saw two guards standing outside the forbidden room, the room where Elizabeth had told him Jacobson held his most precious coat. The door was surely unlocked, as Elizabeth had said, but Gregor didn't know what to do with those two guards.

He knew them, but he knew they didn't like him. If they saw him out at night, they'd probably take him somewhere, lock him up and not let him out for a while. That's what they always did with "security threats" that worked in the house.

There was a mild lighting coming from the ceiling. This was obviously a special corridor if the light now stayed on all night.

"Who are you?" a voice whispered from behind him.

Gregor jumped and yelped, and immediately the two guards' heads snapped in the noise's direction. They started to run towards Gregor. Gregor couldn't see where that voice had come from, but he knew the guards had heard him. He started to run back down the stairs from where he came, and both guards came sprinting around the corner, spotting Gregor and following him down the stairs.

"Red alert! Red alert!" one of the guards started screaming. They ran past the paintings on the walls, and they ran past the two houseplants in the dark edges of the corridor where the light didn't reach.

Martin watched them run by.

"Now the coast is clear," Geraldo said.

"Thanks," Martin said to the newest plant he had met that evening, and he let go of one of its leaves.

The plant didn't respond, and Martin started to gently run round to the room that the guards had been standing at.

"I didn't mean to make him jump," Martin said to Geraldo. "Who was he?"

"He was someone looking for the coats. But his energy was darker than yours. He wanted it for vengeance. The coat would have probably liked him. It draws whoever it can so that it can create some damage."

Martin approached the door. He pushed it open.

A guard was sitting there, in front of a long black coat that stood beneath a grand painting of a man in a suit that looked a bit like Jacobson.

Martin could see the guard was asleep.

"What shall I do with him?" Martin thought.

"Walk behind him," Geraldo said.

Martin walked behind the guard, creeping slowly.

"Remove his weapon."

Martin took the gun from the guard's waist.

"And his knife."

Martin took the knife from his beltline too.

"Now place them on the ground, and pick up the guard."

"Pick him up? I can't, he's a fully grown..."

"Just do it," Geraldo said. "You're stronger than you realise."

Martin squatted down and wrapped his large hands around the chair beneath the guard, who was beginning to snore. Martin pressed through the ground with his legs, and as if he was picking up a cardboard box, the man in his chair was lifted off the ground.

"Goodness," Martin thought.

"Now place him outside the room, come back in and close the door," Geraldo said. Martin did as he was told. The guard was gently placed outside the room, still unconscious, and Martin closed the door as he walked back in.

Martin stared at the coat. He wanted to follow every bit of advice Geraldo had for him now. He was learning to use Geraldo rather than ignoring him sometimes.

"Now what?" Martin said.

"Now take the coat. But don't put it on."

Martin walked up to the coat, reached out, and the coat began to scream.

"No! No!"

Martin recoiled slightly. He could not see a mouth, or eyes, but a dark voice was starting to erupt out of the centre of this coat, which was wrapped around the body of a headless plastic frame.

Martin felt as if the coat was speaking directly into his mind instead of out loud.

"Leave me be!" it yelled. "I have called someone to me, and it is not you! He should be here soon, I could sense him. He was so close!"

"You have to come with me," Martin said.

Everything went silent.

"Is that my brother, and my sister you are wearing?" the coat said. "How dare you? How dare you wear two coats at once! You must think that you can wear *me* now, do you? Well you can't, you absolutely can't! You look more like a plant than a man to me. I serve men, real men who want justice and revenge, not empty, soulless plantmen who have no desire to fix the world or what has happened to them."

Martin just looked at Geraldo. Geraldo was very quiet now.

Martin reached out again to take the coat.

"No! No do not touch me!"

Martin looked at Geraldo. Geraldo nodded.

As soon as Martin touched the coat, he was flooded with darkness. Every foul memory he ever had came rushing to the surface, things he had not thought about for a while. There were memories of Arthur Muldridge and his bullying, there were memories of Jacobson Muldridge before he was demonstralised by Nerris. There were memories of his father, memories of what Martin's father used to be like before he...

Martin wanted to put the coat on. If he could just put the coat on, then everything would be fixed, adequate punishment would be taken out on the people that deserved it...

"Forgiveness is never the answer," he heard the coat say. "And wouldn't you like to see your father again? You can bring him back with my help, you know, but you will have to do some serious damage if you want to..."

"No!" Martin heard Geraldo cry. "No, you are the only one who can fix this. The coat must be taken to the forest to meet with its maker. Do not put it on. You mustn't!"

Martin was looking around for Geraldo, but Martin couldn't see him.

"He isn't real," the coat said. "That bird is just your imagination. I am real. I am the one you should follow. I am the one with the power and knowledge. What has the bird ever done? How has he ever really helped? Can he bring your father back? Can he repay the pain that has been dealt to you by the evil ones in your life? Isn't it time to take control, to really resolve things properly so that all debts of pain are settled?"

Martin couldn't even hear Geraldo anymore. There was something so powerful running through him that every thought of the Garganfan or his mother that tried to emerge into his mind was swiftly brushed away and covered by something so dark that Martin was losing sight of who he was.

He just wanted to wear that coat.

"It will all be over. Every ounce of pain or struggle you have ever felt will be finished with once you just put me on. I see now what we can do together. I was wrong about you before, you are strong. You, me, my brother and my sister. Let us unite, let us become one."

Martin felt his arm raising to put on the coat. He saw in his mind what he would be able to do. He would have enough power to do absolutely anything he wanted...

"Yes," the coat said, "now just put me on."

As Martin took the coat with the other hand, he heard something crashing in through the window behind him.

The Garganfan rolled in and snatched the coat away from Martin so that the connection was lost.

Geraldo appeared again, the room seemed brighter to Martin, and the coat was beginning to melt into the Garganfan's hand and creep its darkness up towards the Garganfan's head and heart.

"Quickly!" the Garganfan said. "Back to the forest. We have to take it to its maker!"

*

"I'm sorry!" Martin cried out as he sprinted after the Garganfan back into the woods. He could hear shouts and cries of guards behind them as they ran, but they were running so fast that the guards were losing sight of them.

"I'm sorry," Martin said to Geraldo, who was flying alongside him.

"You didn't put the coat on, so it's okay," Geraldo said.

"But I nearly did, I was about to, but..."

"Stop thinking about the past!" the Garganfan shouted. "This coat wants to take me over! I have so much pain in my past and ancestry, it's trying to use it."

Martin saw the forest light up with a bright blue that was shining out of the Garganfan's chest, the ancient protective stone seemed to come to life and make the path clear.

"What's happening?" the Garganfan said. "What is this?"

"He needs to jump through whatever the stone shows him," Geraldo said to Martin. "It's a shortcut to the maker of the coats."

"Geraldo says you need to follow it, jump through whatever it shows you, it's a shortcut to the maker!" Martin shouted.

His mother was now running alongside him. He could feel a healing light shining off her and starting to ease all of his own guilt for nearly putting on that coat.

Ahead of them in the blue light, there formed a giant, golden tree with a little man at the base, stooped and hunched over a workbench, building something.

"You have to jump into it!" Martin yelled out, and so the Garganfan did. He jumped in, Martin did too, and Amanda and Geraldo leapt in after the both of them, and soon the blue light had disappeared, and all that could be heard were the shouts of guards and alarm bells ringing from the estate of Jacobson Muldridge.

Trust

*Having someone you can trust in your life
is always something to be grateful for.*

Chapter 6 - Hinzen's Mind

"They will know by now. My master, Quen, will know that you've captured me. He will not let me back anywhere near the compound."

"How do you know?" Kuyasaki said.

Kuyasaki, Myasako and Takashi were standing outside their dojo. They were with the little suited man named Hinzen, who Myasako and Takashi had removed from Quen's underground lair, where Quen's teams of scientists were developing powerful and vicious mutant dogs to support his aims.

Kuyasaki did not want to let Hinzen inside the dojo. He still didn't fully trust him.

"Because I know," Hinzen said. "I know my master."

"You are still calling him your master."

"He has been my master for years! I would love to be able to help you if I could, to help to stop the evil he is planning, but..."

"He lies," Takashi thought. Kuyasaki heard his thought, and so did Myasako. This man was not trustworthy at all. Even if he managed to get into the compound where they were breeding mutant dogs to go in and attack the Great Wolves Of Japan, this man would probably compromise the ninjas' location.

"Now I'm not sure what to do with him," Kuyasaki thought.

"We have to wipe his memory of our whereabouts," Takashi said. "We have to wipe it completely from the time we first spoke to him at the Seishin Mountain. He should have no memory of us."

All of this conversation was going on in the realm of thought. Hinzen was not at all aware of it, but for the first time, Myasako could hear his father and Takashi speak through thought so clearly and easily, that he wondered how often this happened in the past without him realising.

"Very well," Kuyasaki said. "Show Myasako the process in case he ever needs it. I need to meditate on all of this. The great wolves and Nayla are in danger. I do not think we have long before Quen unleashes the dogs on them in an attempt to make them his slaves."

Hinzen began to speak again.

"Just one bite from one of those dogs could make a wolf become just like it, but even more powerful, and totally loyal to master Quen," Hinzen said. He was smiling slightly without realising. "It is quite genius, when you think about it, in his attempt to form his new government where everyone must pay him taxes. But unfortunately he will have divorced me from his plans as soon as he discovered I was taken away by ninjas."

"Very well," Kuyasaki said. "We cannot use you. Takashi will help you find your way back home. We have transport over by the Seishin Mountain. Takashi and Myasako will take you there so that you can return to your life as you see fit."

Hinzen looked at Kuyasaki, slightly stunned. Surely this had been too easy.

"Really?" Hinzen said. "I'm free to go? You don't want to use me anymore?"

"We can't," Kuyasaki said. "As you have already explained. You are no use to us if your master does not trust you anymore. You will not be able to access any of his plans or territory."

"No," Hinzen agreed, slightly frantically. "No, he wouldn't let me near him now."

"Then farewell," Kuyasaki bowed.

"Farewell," Hinzen imitated, and Takashi took the man by the arm, beckoned Myasako with a slight turn of his head, and the three of them walked off towards the Seishin Mountain behind the dojo, in the distance.

*

When Takashi, Hinzen and Myasako arrived at the base of the Seishin Mountain, Takashi began to pull Hinzen behind him as he and Myasako began to climb upwards.

"Where are we going?" Hinzen said. "The transport. Where is the transport that your master mentioned?"

"Up here," Takashi muttered.

"He doesn't speak much," Myasako reassured Hinzen. He didn't want Hinzen to start rebelling.

"What is your name?" Hinzen said to Myasako.

Takashi glared at Myasako in warning.

"Ferama," Myasako said. "My name is Ferama."

"Well, Ferama," Hinzen said, "how long have you been training as a ninja?"

At that moment Takashi snatched Hinzen off his feet by pulling sharply at his arm. He pinned Hinzen to the wall of the mountain.

"No questions," Takashi hissed. Myasako could tell that Takashi would rather cut the man's head off than send him away safely, but he knew that Kuyasaki would never allow such a thing.

"We could end his life, if we had to," Takashi thought.

"No," Myasako said. "You know that's not right. You are the one letting your emotions get the better of you now."

Takashi loosened his grip around Hinzen's throat, who had tears in his eyes.

"Perhaps," Takashi thought. "I seek efficient elimination of dangers and threats. This man serves evil. I would rather see him ended if I had the choice."

Myasako was silent.

"But of course, Kuyasaki is a wiser man than me," Takashi admitted. Then Myasako noticed a pause in Takashi's mind, while Takashi really considered if Kuyasaki would be right in this instance.

"Let's go," Takashi said, and he continued to lead Hinzen up the mountain, to the dwelling of the Mind Melder.

Lead

If you do not feel comfortable,
do not blindly follow what others do.

Chapter 7 - The Mind Melder

The Mind Melder lived alone in an unknown part of the Seishin Mountain that stood facing away from the dojo, towards the forest. It was said that the Mind Melder enjoyed the view of the forest, rather than the town.

"Where are we going?" Hinzen said again. He was beginning to look worried as he was still pulled by Takashi up the mountain. They began to walk around a very thin ledge that led to the other side. Myasako was following behind them.

"We are nearly there," Myasako said, trying to keep Hinzen quiet. Takashi refused to speak.

"But where are we going?" Hinzen repeated.

"I don't actually know," Myasako said. "But I'm sure it's safe."

"I thought I was going to be transported home! What could possibly be up here?"

Hinzen began to struggle, trying to break free from the grip that Takashi had on his forearm. He was unable to shift it.

"Let me go! Let me go!"

Hinzen lifted his arm to strike down on Takashi's clasping hand, when Takashi turned towards him, looked down at the ground, and quickly pulled the man's body towards himself, so that Hinzen's chin crashed into the top of Takashi's head.

Myasako saw the man's body go limp, and Takashi picked him up and put him on his own shoulder.

"It was necessary," Takashi said, looking at Myasako before he continued to walk again. "He will wake again soon."

When Takashi and Myasako had walked around to the other side of the mountain, there was a very narrow gap, only wide enough for one body at a time.

"I will go first," Takashi said. "Feed his arms and body through so that I may drag Hinzen to the other side."

"Okay," Myasako said. Even though the small gap in the mountain looked dark and ominous, like something no one should enter, Myasako trusted that Takashi knew what he was doing.

Takashi crawled, quickly but silently through the gap, and Myasako pushed Hinzen's small body, arms first, on his back, through the gap so that Takashi could grab it on the other side.

Once Hinzen's body began to be dragged through, Myasako crawled in and followed after.

When Myasako stood up again inside a cave of the mountain, it was shining with blue light. He looked around and could see nothing except a small ape-like figure that was wearing a loincloth, sitting by itself at the other side of the cave, emanating a blue and slightly golden light while it had its eyes closed.

"Kneel before the Mind Melder," Takashi thought. Myasako heard him clearly, and as they kneeled, Hinzen began to wake up.

"Where am I?" Hinzen said. "My chin hurts. What's that thing? Is that a monkey?"

The Mind Melder had not moved. It had not even opened its eyes.

Takashi actually began to speak out loud.

"We request that this man's memory be erased since the time of our arrival at the base of the Seishin Mountain, just two hours ago," Takashi said. He leant forward and touched his forehead to the floor of the cave.

"We request this because he may give away our whereabouts to the people that seek to do evil in this world."

Suddenly the Mind Melder opened its eyes and a fierce blue light shot out of them, which went directly into Hinzen's eyes. Hinzen's body froze, his face became taught, and he was slowly lifted off the ground.

"This man is a slave of evil," the Mind Melder said. The Mind Melder had a deep booming voice that Myasako could feel vibrating the bones in his chest.

"This man's mind deserves to be completely wiped away! Do you request this, too – a complete melding of his mind with the very Earth beneath him, so all that he has is the knowledge of the trees and the plants and the air and the sky?"

Takashi was not sure. It would be going further than Kuyasaki ordered, but surely it would be best if...

"Yes! Release me from evil!" Hinzen yelled out. His voice sounded desperate and pleading as he remained hovering in mid-air, now engulfed in an orb of blue light. "Release me from the burden of evil! I can taste the freedom! Do it!"

"Very well," the Mind Melder said. The Mind Melder closed his eyes, Hinzen dropped to the ground, and Myasako saw a dark, wretched red energy begin to lift from Hinzen's mind, and it went upwards into the cave above him.

"This man is reset to become in tune with the Earth around him!" the Mind Melder yelled, and suddenly Hinzen was thrown up high into the cave and then sucked into the rocks above them so that only his face was visible to Myasako.

"Goodbye!" Hinzen smiled, and as his face disappeared completely, the Mind Melder opened its eyes again and Hinzen's body dropped back down to the ground, and he sat up as the Mind Melder watched him. Now all the light that was left was the blue golden light coming from the body of the Mind Melder. Hinzen stood up.

"My name is Hinzen," Hinzen said. "I have knowledge of the forest so deep and powerful that many others may not ever experience it. I am happy to serve the cause of good. May I serve you? You seem to support the cause of good."

Takashi stood to his feet.

"Perhaps there are ways you can help us now," Takashi bowed. "Thank you."

Hinzen bowed back. Myasako saw he was in his purest form, an intelligent man without a trace of resistance or evil. Now he just wanted to do good.

Everyone looked at the Mind Melder, who once again had its eyes closed, and wasn't moving at all.

*

"Does he really remember nothing?" Myasako said to the Mind Melder after a few minutes of sitting. "It would be really helpful if he could remember a few things about a man named Quen, and what he plans to do in the forest."

"He will receive useful knowledge when necessary, but he will not be able to keep it," the Mind Melder said. It still had its eyes closed. "This man is clean enough inside to receive memories that serve his now good intentions. But the memories will not live in him. They will leave him as soon as possible."

Myasako looked at Hinzen. Hinzen almost had the look of a baby on his face. Completely innocent and empty, without a past or any preconceptions about the world or its inhabitants.

"Who is Quen?" Hinzen asked.

"You will remember, when needed," the Mind Melder said.

*

After the meeting with the Mind Melder was ended, all three of its visitors crawled out of its dwelling and stood up on the side of the mountain, overlooking the forest in the distance.

Hinzen suddenly took a deep, sharp breath in as he looked towards the trees.

"Bad things will happen there, we must stop it. We must stop it. Huge dogs, huge dogs will come and attack and enslave. We must stop it."

Hinzen began to look around.

"We must leave the mountain. We must go to the forest. I know the direction they will come from."

Hinzen was itching to move. "How do we get down?!"

"Follow me," Takashi said, and instead of dragging Hinzen after him, Takashi hoisted the man over his shoulder again, and began to sprint around the mountain to run down its side, in the direction of Kuyasaki and the dojo.

*

"The forest! The forest! We must get to the forest!" Hinzen was yelling on Takashi's back as they made it around the side of the mountain.

"We must await our master," Takashi said, and as he did so, Myasako could see his father running towards them. Takashi must have called him through thought.

Kuyasaki was so fast that the small figure of the man soon became a large one, and he was almost flying up the mountainside to meet with his son, Takashi and Hinzen.

"Hinzen is cleaned," Kuyasaki said, seeming to know everything that had already happened.

"We must get to the forest!" Hinzen was still on Takashi's shoulders.

"Then let us go. Myasako. Take Hinzen up to the cave of transportation, the same cave we entered when we first infiltrated your uncle Senzi's compound together."

"Why can't we just go straight there, the same way you made us just vanish from Senzi's compound when we had to leave?" Myasako said.

"Me and Takashi have one more thing to do. You must practice your own skills. We will meet you in the forest."

"What do you have to do?" Myasako said.

"I will not say. It came to me in meditation. You are too young to join us. I have risked your safety before. I will not do it again."

"But if I'm going with you to fight Quen and his dogs, you are already putting me at risk!"

"This is the life of the ninja. Your help is needed, but you are simply not developed enough to join me and Takashi in this just yet. All will become clear. Please, do as I say. Go to Nayla, meet with the wolves. Tell them of what is to come. We will be with you soon."

Myasako wanted to rebel and follow his father and Takashi to wherever they were going.

"It is safer for you this way," Kuyasaki said. "We will see you soon."

Kuyasaki placed his hand on Takashi's shoulder, and the two of them disappeared into nothing.

Unity

*Merging your mind with the Earth
connects you with a fresh intelligence.*

Chapter 8 - The Ancient Warlord

Takashi and Kuyasaki appeared beside each other in the deepest part of the mountain. Takashi had never seen it before. It was dark and warm.

"What is this place?" Takashi thought.

"It is the heart of the Seishin Mountain," Kuyasaki said. "I saw it arise as a vision within me during meditation. I was instructed to bring you here with me. But I do not know why."

They both heard a rummaging around in the darkness. There was a groaning.

"Who goes there?" came a deep and growling voice from the shadows.

"My name is Kuyasaki, this is Takashi. We are ninjas from beyond the mountain."

"Ninjas! I hate ninjas! How could I hear you if you are supposed to be ninjas! Ninjas are supposed to be absolutely silent!"

"We do not wish to creep up on you," Kuyasaki reassured the dark voice. "I was instructed to come here whilst in meditation. Is this your home?"

There was a pause as Kuyasaki heard a clinking of metal, more groaning, and the shuffling sounds of something very large standing to its feet.

"This has been my home for hundreds of years. Few ever visit me."

"Why here?" Kuyasaki asked.

There was one more groan, and footsteps began to slightly shake the stony ground beneath the ninjas' feet.

"I was cursed. Sent here by my old master after I betrayed him in battle. I wanted his armour. I tried to kill him so that I could steal it. There were ferocious wolves we were battling against at one time. We were trying to enslave them to make them our own. I was told that I would be sent to the heart of the mountain until I could repay my debt and serve some form of good. Anyone who has come here has never been able to defeat me."

"Defeat you?" Kuyasaki asked. "If your task is to do good, why do you fight those who come to see you?"

As Kuyasaki and Takashi's eyes quickly began to adjust to the darkness around them, they could see who they were talking to. They could feel its footsteps as it drew itself further in. It looked like a huge, armoured Samurai with a sword in its metallic hand. Kuyasaki and Takashi could see this warrior's yellow eyes, and he was twice the size of Kuyasaki.

"That is the breed of ancient warlord," Takashi said. "They were bred to invade and take over entire civilisations."

"I am indeed bred for battle!" the ancient warlord cried. "All I know is how to fight. And now I have my chance to perhaps serve my master well. He tells me, even now, that you ninjas are looking to actually *protect* those same species of wolves that we battled against all those years ago. If I can stop you, perhaps the great master Quen, a descendent of my own master, will help bring back true balance to our people."

Now that some time had passed, Kuyasaki and Takashi were completely at home. They had been trained from young ages to learn to do everything in the dark, even better than they could in broad daylight.

"Let battle commence!" the ancient warlord cried, and Takashi drew his daggers as Kuyasaki drew his sword.

The ancient warlord was fast and powerful. Already he was slicing and slashing at Kuyasaki's throat, and Kuyasaki did not try to block any of the strikes with his own sword. He felt as if the ancient warlord's sword would cut straight through his own, so his instincts took over, and instead Kuyasaki dodged, ducked, rolled, and began to move closer in towards the warlord's body.

Takashi was fully tapped in to the same intelligence that guided him through the darkness of the forest when he went to help Myasako and Nayla at the Akuma Mountain, but now it was mixed with the pure, ferocious desire of protectiveness that would arise whenever Kuyasaki was threatened. Takashi flanked the ancient warlord and instinctively threw a dagger up towards the warlord's neck.

It managed to cut in through a thin slant between the warlord's helmet and body armour, and both ninjas heard a squelching sound as the dagger went deep into its throat.

They heard the warlord gasp. There was a pause in the striking and slashing.

The ninjas took their chance. With his one remaining dagger, Takashi could find the knees of the ancient warlord and drive his dagger upwards where the knee armour met with the shin armour. Takashi could feel he was cutting ligaments in half.

The ancient warlord cried out and dropped to his knees. He quickly swung his sword around at Takashi, who knew it was coming already. Takashi ducked and rolled and climbed up the warlord's kneeling body so that he could regain his other dagger.

He could not see where Kuyasaki was.

He snatched his dagger from the warlord's bleeding neck, and the warlord reached up to grab at Takashi's clinging body.

"Get off me!" the warlord cried.

Takashi moved out of the way of the swiping hand, but soon the other one was swiping, and as Takashi slipped on the bleeding armour beneath his feet, he managed to drive his dagger into another part of the warlord's neck.

The warlord screamed. Takashi slid down the warlord's body, and Kuyasaki was standing behind him.

"We must take the sword," Kuyasaki said. "Together."

Takashi ran around to the front of the warlord, and the warlord began swinging its sword around the ground in an attempt to keep the ninjas at bay.

Takashi jumped over a swipe, and managed to cling on to the warlord's wrist for a moment.

Kuyasaki cast a very thin climbing cable from his waist up towards the warlord's neck. It lodged in between its plates of armour, and Kuyasaki pulled and launched himself up to the shoulders and began to wrap the cable around the warlord's throat.

The warlord let go of its sword and reached up with both hands to pull Kuyasaki away from his neck.

Takashi let go of the wrist, dropped to the ground, and began to drag the heavy sword into the furthest corner of the cave.

"I have you! I can feel you!" the warlord cried, and as he went to throw Kuyasaki's body into the wall of the mountain, Kuyasaki stayed clung on to the cable that tightened as he was thrown across the cave.

Kuyasaki didn't hit the wall, but snapped back onto the warlord's body as the cable went tight, and the warlord began to choke.

The warlord began to gasp and cling and scratch at its throat.

"I don't want to die like this. Not in this place! Not in the darkness!"

Kuyasaki was holding the cable tight. Takashi was now watching, ready for anything else to come.

"I pledge..." the warlord gasped. "I pledge allegiance to you, master."

Suddenly the darkness lifted, and light seemed to emerge from the ground, and the figure of an even larger warlord appeared, standing beside the bleeding and choking one.

This warlord seemed ethereal, golden and slightly shimmering. It was not moving, but was looking down at the bleeding warlord on the floor.

"We were wrong to enslave," the new, bright, golden warlord said. "This is your final mission in this life, Golhara, to correct our mistakes and bring true harmony back between the wolf and human worlds. On pledging allegiance to the master Kuyasaki, you have promised to serve and give your life for his cause. And on carrying out this mission, your freedom will be given."

The golden warlord knelt down, touched his younger apprentice, and Kuyasaki felt his cable untie around its throat, and Takashi could see the shining red over the warlord's armour begin to evaporate.

The warlord's breathing calmed down. The air calmed down. Takashi saw the warlord's sword at the wall of the cave shoot back towards its armoured hand, then the warlord stood, as its old master disappeared into the ether.

The ancient warlord took a deep breath.

"I am renewed. My name is Golhara. I am one of the descendents of the Great Ferokuma, the most powerful warlord of any known time. He has given me his blessing, his promise of freedom. And now I am ready to serve you, Master Kuyasaki."

The ancient warlord named Golhara dropped to one knee, bowed his head with his sword by his side, and Takashi did the same, dropping to one knee, facing Kuyasaki, holding his daggers at his waist.

"And now we are ready for war," Kuyasaki said.

War

Freedom from war is a tremendous freedom.

Chapter 9 - Preparation

Myasako had been leading Hinzen up the Seishin Mountain, towards the cave of transportation.

Myasako stopped.

"What is it?" Hinzen said.

"I don't know," Myasako said. "My father, I feel as if he has been fighting."

"I'm sure he's fine," Hinzen said. "Takashi seems like a ferocious warrior. Surely the two of them will be fine together."

"Yeh," Myasako said, looking around to the dojo behind him. "Yeh, I hope so."

When the two arrived at the portal of transport – the pool of green water in the ground of a cave in the side of the mountain, Hinzen stared into it.

"Now what?" Hinzen said.

Myasako explained. He explained to Hinzen that they had to hold a vision of where they wanted to be, and then the water would take them directly there.

"Really?" Hinzen said. "Very well. Let's do it."

"We want to stick together," Myasako said. "We want to appear in the forest in sight of Nayla and the great dark wolves. We don't want to startle them. We want to appear far enough away so that they don't suddenly attack us."

"Very well," Hinzen said. "Not so close that they don't suddenly attack us."

Hinzen crouched in preparation to jump into the water. Myasako realised what Hinzen had just said, and what he was now focussing on with the majority of his mind.

"No! Wait!" Myasako said, but before Hinzen could stop himself, he was in mid-air, eager to serve and do his part, and he was falling into the green water beneath him, now fully focussed on being so close to the wolves that he might be attacked.

Hinzen disappeared and the water flashed green. Myasako had to steady his mind.

"Now I need to stay with Hinzen to keep him safe," Myasako said. "He is to help us on our mission, so I must follow him to keep him safe."

Myasako held his intent and jumped, hit the water and soon the world was bright green again. Everything happened quickly, his vision was so pure that he could see Hinzen ahead of him, being dragged through some kind of portal, but the few seconds' delay meant that Hinzen had appeared in the forest without Myasako, right beside a wolf. Myasako could see the wolf turn and grab Hinzen in its mouth.

The forest fully materialised around Myasako.

"Wait!" Myasako said. "Wait! Wait don't kill him! He's a friend."

Myasako was amongst a circle of wolves. Luckily they recognised him. Nayla was nearby. She growled at one of the wolves. The wolf released Hinzen, and Hinzen fell to the ground.

"Oh, what happened!" Hinzen said, standing to his feet and noticing his arms were bleeding. "I thought I was supposed to focus on not being close enough to be attacked by those wolves."

"But you were focussing on what you didn't want," Myasako said. "You were focussing on the dangers rather than the safety. You were focussing on what you wanted to avoid rather than what you wanted to achieve. What you focussed on became your reality. Next time we must make distance and safety our main intention, rather than focussing on danger and risk."

"Oh," Hinzen said. "Okay. Very well then." He was still dusting himself off. "So what now?"

"Now we have to explain what has been happening so that Nayla and the wolves can get ready," Myasako said.

*

As Myasako explained what Quen had been planning underground, and as Nayla translated his words to the wolves, one of the wolves began to lick Hinzen's wounds. Hinzen nearly fell over from the force at first.

"Try not to resist," Nayla said. "They still have lake water in their mouths, so it will heal you quickly."

Myasako noticed that he could not see the lake or the local village anywhere nearby. Nayla saw him looking around.

"We all needed some space," she said. "We may be developing peace between our worlds, but I don't think the villagers will want to try to help us fight against these dogs that are coming."

"They might when they realise what will happen if even one of your wolves gets bitten," Myasako said.

He looked at Hinzen. Hinzen's eyes seemed to pop with brightness for a moment. A memory entered his head.

"Any wolf bitten by the mutant dogs will become loyal to Quen, and twice as powerful," Hinzen said. The wolf stopped licking him and Myasako saw that his bleeding arms were now covered in fresh, unbroken skin.

Nayla looked as if she was getting tense. Myasako saw her clenching her fists.

"Will it ever end?" she said to the ground, and then to Myasako. "Will the fighting ever stop? Will there ever be peace?"

"I hope so," Myasako said. "But do you really want it to end? You have to look at yourself. How quick are you to want to fight?"

"Very quick," Nayla said. "I want to destroy anything that threatens us."

"And do you like it?" Myasako said.

Nayla looked at the ground again.

"Yes," she said. "Yes, I like it. I love justice. I love vengeance. I love the idea of payback."

Myasako saw dark clouds start to form above the forest, as if Nayla was somehow summoning them with her mind.

"Hang on," Myasako said. "Is that you?"

"What?" Nayla said. Her concentration on the love of war and justice was broken for a moment, and she looked at Myasako with more clarity in her eyes. The clouds parted slightly.

"I think your powers are growing, ever since you've had those possessions by the Wolf Witches," Myasako said. "I think you are affecting the weather."

"How?" Nayla said.

"I don't know, but when you were focussing on war, everything was getting darker."

Nayla looked at the ground again, and Myasako heard a thunderstorm.

"I do feel them," Nayla said. "They keep wanting to use me. They keep filling me with energy, thoughts of fight and battle and justice for the wolves."

"But those are the kinds of thoughts that can draw war towards you!" Myasako said. "It's the same as with the cave of transportation – what you focus on can become your reality."

"No," Nayla said in a darker, deeper voice. "No. If they come with war, then we will give them war. We will give them war so severe that they will not be able to even consider any kind of battle ever again. Whoever comes to us will be slain. Whoever seeks to bite my wolves will be punished."

Myasako noticed a distant flash of lightning and another rumble of thunder.

"When will they be here?" Myasako said to Hinzen. "And when will they come?"

"Soon," Hinzen said. "I'll show you where."

*

The wolves were running through the woods. Three of them carried Myasako, Hinzen and Nayla on their backs.

"How many dogs will they bring?" Nayla said as the pack of wolves ran through the woods.

Hinzen's eyes popped with brightness again.

"At least forty," he said.

"Forty?" Myasako yelled. "I only saw ten when I snuck into the compound."

"But the compound is large," Hinzen said. "We do not keep large numbers together in case they somehow manage to join forces and break away from their cages."

"But you said they were loyal to Quen," Nayla said.

"Yes," Hinzen said, almost as if he was accessing another life in his memory. "Yes but these animals are still new breeds. They are not completely reliable. We did not want to take risks. When they are unleashed in battle, Quen will be nearby, and they are indoctrinated to serve him. If they can smell him, they will certainly stay loyal."

"Quen will be close?" Nayla said. "Not hiding away in some cave?"

Hinzen shook his head. "If he's not close, then he runs the risk of the dogs losing their loyalty to him. We have never had them out together in the wild before..."

The thundering had stopped. Nayla was more focussed on the task at hand, with less emotion pumping through her veins. Myasako could still feel a certain darkness in the air.

"And how do we know where you think they will enter the forest is correct?" Nayla said. "What if they have changed their plans?"

Hinzen was quiet.

"There is always that risk," he said. "The attack has been planned for months, but now that I am free, now that they know I might have been cleansed...perhaps their plans will have changed."

Myasako suddenly felt a shakiness take over his heart. He felt his sense of control over the situation starting to slip.

His father's voice appeared in his mind as it sometimes would:

"The only control you have is over how you feel. You must seek clarity and wisdom."

Myasako took a deep breath in, a deep breath out, and hoped that Kuyasaki and Takashi would soon appear alongside him, in the forest.

制
御

Control

*Your primary control
is over how you think and feel.*

Chapter 10 - The Coatmaker's Kin

When Martin, Amanda, the Garganfan and Geraldo all landed after jumping through the blue light that appeared out of the Garganfan's chest, it was not night time anymore. It was light. They were in another forest. The tree standing ahead of them was certainly the largest tree Martin had ever seen. It still had a golden tinge, but it was not as golden as it had first appeared.

The Garganfan was struggling to let go of the coat. Martin could see strain on the Garganfan's face as he stood to his feet.

The darkness leaking out of the coat was now so close to the Garganfan's heart, it was like a large finger about to touch the stone in his chest.

"Aggghh!" the Garganfan yelled.

Amanda stood to her feet to help, and as she approached, the darkness touched the stone in the Garganfan's chest. As soon as it touched, the stone grew so bright that Martin and Amanda had to shut their eyes. The brightness seemed to flood through the entire forest and make everything go white.

When the flash had faded, Martin opened his eyes to see the coat on the ground beside the Garganfan, released, and the Garganfan was back to normal.

"There is still more I am to learn about my own heart," the Garganfan said. "Luckily for me, it seems incorruptible. Without it in my chest, without you having brought it back from Japan, Martin, I would have certainly become corrupted by that coat. The desire for vengeance, the desire to wage war and revisit past wars was so strong that I...I am lucky to have the heart that I now I have. Thank you."

"Well thanks for saving *me*," Martin said. "That coat nearly took me over completely. How did you know to come crashing in? Why didn't you just do that in the first place?"

"Something moved me," the Garganfan said. "I thought you had it under control, until the strongest urge seemed to move up from the ground, launch me across Jacobson's land, and I was able to jump so high that I plummeted in through the window that I could see some movement in. I didn't know why I was doing it, but the urge and the power was undeniable. I couldn't control it."

"Instinct," Geraldo said, as he listened while sitting beside Martin. "He's totally in tune with the Earth's intelligence."

"Well thanks again," Martin said. "I was so close to..."

"Don't worry," the Garganfan said. "Just don't touch it again."

81

The Garganfan, Amanda and Martin looked around for the man they had seen in the image of light in the forest. They could see no one.

"Is this a different time?" Martin said. "I thought you said Garganfans couldn't time travel."

"That's what I was always told, but I had learnt from Garganfans who did not have the heart that I now have. Perhaps this has changed things." The Garganfan touched the stone in his chest. It was now so fused within his body, it seemed it could never be removed.

"When you lost your heart the first time," Martin said, feeling his curiosity start to take him over, "all those years ago...you've never spoken about it. Can you remember it? Can you remember everything now, how it happened, how you lost it?"

The Garganfan looked around.

"Yes," he said. "But that is a story for another time. Right now we must focus on the mission at hand. I heard the Earth say that the coat must go back to its maker, but I do not know who made these coats. I was just following where my feet led, and then your words encouraged me to jump into this...place. I don't recognise it, but the energy of this forest seems familiar."

"We are no longer in England," Geraldo said. "We are in Japan. This is part of the Shinwa Forest, a deep, unknown part of the forest that gave birth to these three coats."

Martin felt as if he wanted to distance himself from the foreign powers he had been utilising. He slowly took off his coat, which turned into two, a silver and a blue one, and he placed them on the ground beside him. The sensation of slow motion and accelerated time left him completely, and he once again felt normal.

"That's a relief," Martin said. "Those coats were giving me the strangest sensations."

"Who goes there!" came a voice from up above them. "Don't any of you move or I'll blow a dart right into that young man's neck."

Martin slowly looked up and saw the old man from the image of light that they had jumped into, hanging upside-down by his legs from the tree, with a blowpipe in his mouth, pointing it directly at Martin.

Martin wished he hadn't taken off the coats now.

"We come here in peace," the Garganfan said, standing up and raising his arms.

The hanging man looked at the Garganfan, and slowly his blowpipe left his mouth.

"You? It's you? It's really you?" the man said. The old man looked decrepit and weak, but he swung

83

himself through the branches of the huge tree, gripped onto the massive trunk by wrapping his little arms and legs around it as much as he could, and then slid down the tree as if he was a raindrop sliding down a window. He reached the bottom, put his blowpipe in his pocket and held out his hand for the Garganfan to shake.

"You are the King Of The Trees! The King Of The Garganfans!"

The Garganfan shook the man's hand without saying anything.

"I know you! I know you!" the old man said. "My grandfather, he used to tell me about you. He had drawings of you and everything! He said you saved this forest, you sacrificed yourself, you sacrificed your own heart to preserve this place, and you were sent to another land to forget your truth. You remember now, don't you?"

The Garganfan looked slightly confused.

"Well I thought I could remember it, mostly," the Garganfan said. "But I don't remember you."

"Of course not! I wasn't born when you were here. But my grandfather, you must remember him? He was called the Coatmaker. He was an inventor, he used..."

"He used the power of the forest," the Garganfan said. "Yes, yes I remember now. He tried to help, didn't he? But something went wrong..."

The little man looked at Martin, Amanda, and then the coats on the ground.

"Those..." he said. "Are those them? Are they his three original coats?"

The Garganfan nodded. "Yes."

"Good grief!" the little man said, rushing over and picking up the two by Martin's side. He quickly put them on.

Martin looked at the Garganfan. The Garganfan raised his hands to indicate "calm".

"He put a spell on me, you know," the old man said. "My grandfather said that time travel was too much trouble for anyone's own good. He said that the past should be left alone, in the past, never to be meddled with or played about with, so he put me under a spell so that I wouldn't be able to use the coats, even if I wanted."

He walked up to the dark coat. Martin hadn't heard its voice for a while.

"Don't you dare touch me," the coat said to the man. "If you do I'll..."

"Shut up," the little old man said. He smacked the coat with his hand as it lay on the ground, and then he stamped on it with his heel.

The coat seemed to wheeze slightly.

"You're the wrong'un, aren't ya?" the little old man said to the dark coat. "You're the one who went astray, you're the one who made all those problems for us! If it weren't for the Garganfan here, you would have..."

"Destroyed you all," the coat chuckled. "I know, I was so close."

"Quiet," the man said again, smacking the coat with the back of his hand. "I know just what to do with you. My grandfather said if I ever saw you again, with your brother and sister here, then I would know exactly what to do. He prepared me for this day. He always told me it would come."

The old man turned and began to walk towards the large tree.

He tapped lightly with his foot, twice at the base of the trunk. The bottom of the trunk opened up and a stairway led downwards into the Earth.

"I might need your help," the man said, turning to the other three. "My grandfather said whoever had touched the coats last would need to be involved. Follow me. Let's put an end to this troublemaker."

The little old man turned around, didn't look back, and started walking down the staircase that led deeper underground.

Lineage

*Be grateful for the wisdom gained from elders,
and discard what is of no use to you.*

Chapter 11 - The Coatmaker's Lair

As Martin followed the Garganfan down the steps to keep up with this little old man, Amanda followed behind him. Martin realised that now he had taken off those coats, he couldn't see Geraldo anymore.

He wondered if he was still there, right by his side.

After a while of walking through golden-lit stairways that led further and further underground, all four of them reached a wall, with another painting. This was the painting of the Coatmaker. It looked a little bit like the painting that Jacobson had in his house, behind the dark coat, except this man was taller, with coats surrounding him, and the man was wearing the same dark coat that had been kept in Jacobson's house.

"This," the little old man said, "is my grandfather. He was the Coatmaker. The greatest Coatmaker to ever have lived. Grandfather, we request entry, please."

"He's not still alive, is he?" Martin whispered.

"That depends on what you mean by 'alive'," the little old man said.

Very slowly the painting swung back, as if it was an automatic door, and behind it sat a large room, filled with thousands of coats, all stacked up on top of each other.

"These are the coats that never saw the light of day. My grandfather feared that if just one of them was a time-travelling coat, it might fall into the wrong hands again, so he made me promise to never release them into the world."

They walked into the room. There were coats of different styles and colours that Martin had never seen anything similar to before.

"Do the other coats have powers?" Martin said.

"Some do," the little old man said, placing the three new coats on top of the pile. "But it's hard to tell without my grandfather here in person. He speaks to me in dreams sometimes, he lives in these walls, but I can never have conversations with him to see which ones are safe to be released."

"Didn't he know when he made them?" Martin said. "Couldn't he tell at the time?"

The little old man started to laugh.

"Goodness gracious, no, dear boy! No, of course not! He made so many coats in his final days that he could not test them all out. And these coats were like babies to him, he couldn't control how they were born – what talents they had, what their destiny was. He would just make them, and find out later what they could do, if he had the time."

"How did he..." Martin wasn't sure if he should ask.

"How did he die? He put on the wrong coat. He put on that one." The little old man pointed to the dark coat that Martin and the Garganfan had taken from Jacobson's house. "He wore that coat and he couldn't take it off. It led to his demise, and the coat was taken from him by someone else."

"By Jacobson Muldridge's father?" Martin asked, thinking of the painting in the room at the house.

"No. His grandfather. His grandfather took it from my grandfather after it was finished with him. My father always said that I shouldn't go after it, that it would return here when the time was right."

"I shouldn't be here!" the dark coat grumbled. "I should be out there working, setting things right. I could never convince the Muldridge's to put me on after they saw what I did to their own grandfather, but I nearly had the boy..."

"Don't make me smack you again," the little old man said.

Martin looked around at the coats.

"So you've never tried any of these on?" It all looked too tempting to Martin.

"No. I made my father and my grandfather a promise," the little old man said. "They thought if I stumbled across one too powerful, then I would destroy myself just like my grandfather did."

Martin went to touch one of the coats, but his mother held his arm gently to stop him.

"Well how did he make them?" Martin said. "Would they just be born out of the ground or something?"

"Something like that," the old man said. "I'm not allowed to discuss his methods. It's another promise he made me keep. I have been waiting for this day, when the three original coats would return here. Now everything can be put right."

The little old man took a match out of his pocket, and he struck it on the ground so it would light.

"What are you doing?" Martin said.

"These coats must be set ablaze. The power of the original three will destroy all the rest."

"Hang on!" Martin said. He could feel all of the power in the room of these coats. "Wait, wait just a moment, please! Isn't that a tremendous waste?

There is so much power here, so much good could be done."

"They must be destroyed," the little old man said. "There is word that a war is coming, a great battle to take hold of the Shinwa Forest and the power of the great dark wolves within it. If these coats fall into the wrong hands, it could doom the entire planet."

"What war? What battle?" Martin said. The little old man hesitated. He blew out the flame on the match while he explained.

"I have been hearing things," the little old man said. "There are ninjas in these woods, near one of the villages. They have come to help the wolves in battle. There is an evil master, I think his name is Quen, or Ken, and he has a hoard of modified, mutated dogs that are more powerful than any natural born beast in the human kingdom. If they bite a creature, it becomes loyal to Quen. Quen wants to take over, he wants to rule everything, form his own government, and if he gets his dogs to bite these wolves, just once, then the wolves will become loyal to him too, with the same enhancements that these dogs have. I dread to think of the power that a Great Dark Wolf Of Japan would wield if it succumbed to any kind of evil enhancement or modification. They would be such a tremendous force that I fear..."

The little old man took out another match and struck it on the ground to light it again.

"These coats must be dealt with."

"What ninjas?" Martin said, interrupting the man again. "Is it Kuyasaki, Myasako, Takashi?"

"Yes, and the chosen one they call Nayla."

Creation

The creator is a vehicle for the creative force.

Chapter 12 - The Earthcoat

"Please don't," Martin said to the little old man, who was still holding a lighted match. "It is such a waste. I'll never see Geraldo again if you..."

"Who?" the little old man said. "I'm sorry, boy. I have a promise to keep." The little old man threw his match onto the dark coat that the Garganfan and Martin had stolen, and the coat began to scream.

"How dare you! You betray the work of your grandfather! You are a traitor! A traitor with no honour!"

Soon the dark coat was burning, shrivelling, and a single flame began to spread and eat through the rest of the coats, and as the flame spread it grew brighter and brighter until Martin was starting to squint, and the dark coat still remained as a shrivelled mess on the floor. Martin saw the two time-travelling coats he had been wearing explode into even more brightness, and the flame started to eat through every coat in the huge pile, leaving no trace of anything behind.

Finally the now huge bright white flame came back to rest on the dark coat that had nearly taken over Martin.

"I see now," the coat whispered. "This is a beautiful death, and I thank you for my rest." The dark coat gave itself to the flame, the flame became so bright that everyone turned their back, and when the flame disappeared they looked again to see a single coat resting on the floor. It was green, and Martin was sure he could see very small roots come up from the Earth, grab hold of it, and fill it with a green, shining light.

"It worked!" the little old man said. "This is the Earthcoat. And just as my grandfather said, the Earthcoat can only ever be worn by an Earthman."

The little old man stooped down low to pick up the coat. Martin had such a hunger to put it on himself, even if it was just for a second. The desire was not dark like with the coat before. It felt tremendously light.

"I see you are a young Earthman," the little old man said, and he walked up to Martin, presenting the coat to him in both hands. The little old man dropped to one knee.

"My grandfather told me, every day he would tell me, that one day a young Earthman would come, that his services would be needed to protect the forest from invaders, and with two other beings by his side, he would put on the final Earthcoat, and he would fight to carry out his duty."

Martin took the coat in his hands. Suddenly the green light from the coat rushed through his body and seemed to plough his mind's energy directly down into the Earth, so that he could feel the heart of the Earth beating through him.

"Put it on, Martin," Amanda said. "The forest needs you."

And so Martin lifted the coat, put it on, and he was never the same again.

*

After a few moments of silence, Martin was still underground with the Garganfan, his mother, and the little old man that was staring at him, beaming with pride.

"A perfect fit," the little old man said.

Martin felt indestructible.

"There's so much power here," Martin said. "I barely know what to do with it." He could now see Geraldo standing beside the Garganfan, looking quite content, gradually becoming invisible and bowing towards Martin.

"Now here is the secret," the little old man said, getting close to Martin and pointing with one finger directly in Martin's eyes.

"*You* don't use the power. *It* uses you. You are the vehicle for the power to move through. If you treat it like that, everything will be far easier and far more powerful."

"Okay," Martin said. He relaxed, he felt as if he was fully charged with a power that was simply waiting for its services to be required.

"How far away are the ninjas you spoke about?" Martin said.

"Three hours' walk. But with that coat you can create your own transport using the root connections of the trees."

"And can this coat time travel?"

"No," the little old man said. "No. My grandfather always said the Earthcoat takes all of the best properties of the other coats, to establish a connection with the Earth that would normally take you years to develop. It is only because of these threatening circumstances that the coat has formed itself before you."

"Well let's go then," Martin said. "Let's go to Kuyasaki and the others. If we are needed, we must help. But not you, Mum, you need to stay somewhere safe."

"I'm capable of a lot more than you think I am," Amanda said with a quiet certainty.

"No, Mum, I don't want you fighting."

"You don't have a choice," Amanda said. "I have to."

Martin didn't like her saying this. He tightened up, and he felt the power from the coat begin to get choked off from his body.

"Resistance does you no good," the little old man said with a slightly threatening point of his finger. "No use resisting, lad. You must surrender."

"Okay," Martin said, relaxing again, almost feeling as if he could fly if he wanted to. "Let's just go then, to find the ninjas, and the wolves."

"Very well," the little old man said. "Listen to the coat, and it will show you how to transport us quickly through the roots of the trees around us."

"Okay. And what's your name?" Martin said as the little old man led them out of the room, bowing to the painting of his grandfather as he did so.

"My name?" the man said. "Call me Jericho."

Emptiness

Empty of your own ideas for a moment,
life begins to flow through you more fully.

Chapter 13 - Loyalty

In a dark room filled with silence, Quen was sitting in his chair, contemplating what would happen when his army of mutant dogs were unleashed on the Great Dark Wolves Of Japan. He was formulating his next steps, what he would be able to do with all of the extra power that he would soon be able to wield onto the world.

Then there was a knock at his door.

"Sir," his assistant said. She was a young woman named Hinoi. "Sir, there is a slight problem with the dogs."

Quen looked up at her. She could not see much of his face in the darkness but she could see the outline of a jagged black mask, and small white eyes glaring out from underneath it.

"What? What problem?" Quen said, almost beginning to stand. He never usually stood.

"The dogs are growing even more in power," the young woman said, "but they are becoming more and more disobedient. The dogs have been trained and drugged to be so loyal to you, that they are starting to disobey your own staff. They are becoming out of control."

"And they think my presence will fix this?"

"Yes, sir, they are convinced that since they injected your blood into the loyalty serum that the dogs were dosed with when they were young, as well as being sprayed with your scent every time they are fed, it means they are programmed to see you as their leader, or even their father. The venom in their fangs will pass this loyalty trait on to any dark wolf of Japan, along with the power accelerator that has been given to the dogs. But the power is accelerating more rapidly than anticipated. The creatures are close to breaking out of their cages. The team requests your presence immediately, to see if you can gain the dogs' loyalty and lead them into the forest."

"Very well," Quen said. "I planned to lead them anyway once they arrived at the forest, we might as well go straight to them at the compound. Prepare my car, and bring me my war weapons. The great battle will soon be upon us."

"Yes, sir," bowed Hinoi, and she left the room to order the guards to bring her master his weapons, that were stored in a black case in a room that was filled with the armour of Quen's ancestors.

Loyalty

*While loyalty is noble,
it can also be misleading.*

Chapter 14 - The Portal Thieves

Kuyasaki, Takashi and the now loyal ancient warlord named Golhara were all knelt in a circle, still in the deepest, darkest part of the mountain.

"Master, when will we leave? How do we get out of this place?" the ancient warlord said.

Takashi knew to be quiet.

"Soon enough," Kuyasaki said. "But I am having trouble accessing any kind of transportation skill. We are so deep in the mountain, so cut off from the outside air, that my usual power source is not readily accessible. I am not currently sure how to get out of here. I am waiting for an answer."

"I can cut," Golhara said. "I can cut our way to freedom. I was always told by my master that on being sent for my final duty for good, I could cut my way through anything if I needed to. This sword is the greatest in the land. It can cut through stone, rock, even the great Ellinong Trees can be brought down with this sword if needed."

"I hope tree cutting will never be necessary," Kuyasaki said. "But if you cut your way out of this mountain, you might damage it irreparably. We do not want to cause harm to a source of such greatness."

The ancient warlord's sword began to gleam with an orange light. Kuyasaki could see it shining through the sheath at the warlord's waist.

"What is happening?" Kuyasaki said.

"I do not know," Golhara said. "It has never done this before." The ancient warlord withdrew his sword, and the warmth that was emanating from the sword was so strong that Takashi and Kuyasaki both stood and took a step back.

"I was told it could cut through *anything* when the time was right," Golhara said. "Perhaps it can even cut through space."

The ancient warlord held the sword vertically so that his armoured face was shining bright with orange, and as he held the sword out in front of him, he made a horizontal cut in the air. Kuyasaki and Takashi both saw that he made a slice, a dark slice of orange that began to turn into a circle as the warlord started to cut down, to the side, and then up again.

"Where are we to go?" Golhara said, bowing at Kuyasaki. "You are the master."

"We are to go into the Shinwa Forest, to be alongside my son," Kuyasaki spoke into the dark orange circle before them.

They watched as the darkness turned to greenery, and then trees, and then a forest. The forest was full of dark wolves, Myasako, Nayla and Hinzen, standing around discussing something.

"There they are," Kuyasaki said. "We must go." As Kuyasaki stood to his feet to approach the circle, the ancient warlord also stood.

"I should test it, master, for safety."

"No," Kuyasaki said, "no I will go first." He still didn't know if he could trust the warlord enough to leave him alone with his son, Nayla and the wolves.

"Very well, master," the warlord bowed, taking a step back.

Takashi wanted to be the first one to test it, to protect Kuyasaki. He stepped forward, and Kuyasaki put his hand on Takashi's chest.

"Let me," Kuyasaki said. He walked up to the vision of the forest that stood before them, still surrounded with a burning orange colour, and he stepped in.

As soon as he stepped, Takashi saw something flash across the vision and snatch at Kuyasaki's leg.

"Master!" Takashi yelled, and before he could finish calling after Kuyasaki, something dark and wicked had snatched Kuyasaki by the leg, and had dragged him away out of sight.

"It is time for our first battle," the ancient warlord said. "We must save our master."

Takashi ran, leapt into the vision, and hoped that he would be able to see where Kuyasaki was taken to.

*

Takashi landed in the forest, beside the Great Dark Wolves Of Japan. Soon the ancient warlord was standing beside him, and the portal they had travelled through, showing the darkness of the inside of the mountain, began to disappear.

"Kuyasaki was taken," Takashi said to everyone. It was rare that he would speak so loudly. "He was taken by something."

Nayla translated to the wolves. They started to growl.

"Portal thieves," Nayla said. "The wolves say there are portal thieves that work in these woods and take whatever they can."

"Why didn't they take us?" Takashi said. He drew his sword.

"Perhaps all of you would have been too much," Nayla said.

The wolves growled again.

"They work in teams," Nayla said. "The wolves say there might have been a lot of them, even if it looked like one."

"How do we save the master?" the ancient warlord cried. He drew his own sword and it was now shining with silver light.

All of the wolves suddenly bowed. Nayla fell to one knee.

"I know what that is," Nayla said, looking towards the shining sword.

"How?" Myasako said.

"It's in my memory somewhere," Nayla said. "I don't know how. That is the one empowered sword. It is a sword blessed with powers that ordinary swords only wished they had. It was used here once, to help save the wolves from a dire enslavement."

The ancient warlord looked at his sword.

"It was never a blessed sword before," he said, staring at it.

"It's not the sword, specifically," Nayla said, standing to her feet as the wolves did. "It's the power that runs through it. The power flowing through it is the valuable thing, not the sword. The power can move between swords if it wants. It chooses who can wield it."

The ancient warlord lowered his sword.

"Then with all of this power I demand to save the master Kuyasaki!" he cried. He slashed his sword furiously through the air, jumped into the slash he had made, and to everyone else it looked as if he was jumping into complete darkness.

"Stay here, my brother!" he yelled to Takashi, and before Takashi could chase after him and leap through the gap he had made in the air, the gap had closed and Takashi was jumping, only to land on the same ground, beside one of the great dark wolves.

"He is a loyal warrior," Takashi muttered.

*

The ancient warlord was thrown through darkness, but his sword was so bright that he could see the way. In the distance he could see Kuyasaki battling dark, shadowy creatures that were trying to steal his clothes and weapons. He was fighting them off, rolling, evading, but sometimes his feet or fists or daggers would slice through the dark creatures without making any impact. It was as if they were made of the shadows.

"I'm coming, master!" the ancient warlord cried, and as he did, he saw all of the dark shadowy creatures look towards him. "You portal thieves will be slain, just as all the other evil ones have been slain."

Golhara flew into the crowd and began slicing at the creatures with such ferocity that Kuyasaki began to step back and watch. Sometimes Kuyasaki would feel the grip of a creature on his back, or sense that they were about to swipe at him, and he could fend them off with his skills and throw them towards the ancient warlord.

The ancient warlord would see them, slice them, and the dark creatures would begin to evaporate. Their surroundings would become lighter, and Kuyasaki was sure that he could see faint outlines of trees.

He realised that the shadowy creatures could become formless and untouchable, but this also meant that they could not touch him at the same time.

If Kuyasaki felt one grab at him, he could grab them back and keep launching them at Golhara, who's sword was becoming full of so many colours that the shadowy creatures began to run away from it in fear.

The ancient warlord would chase them, grab them or slice at them to make them fall.

Kuyasaki could see the great wolves and Myasako around him.

"We have nearly won, master," Golhara said. "Nearly!"

Kuyasaki kicked a final portal thief towards the ancient warlord, who sliced through it, and suddenly they were both amongst the wolves, Takashi, Myasako, Nayla and Hinzen.

Takashi bowed.

"Thank you," Takashi said to the ancient warlord. Myasako had never seen Takashi show any signs of weakness, but for a moment it was as if Takashi had collapsed onto the ground with relief. Myasako barely knew what had been going on, and in just a matter of seconds, it seemed as if this giant warrior had set everything right.

"Yes, thank you, Golhara," Kuyasaki said, shaking off any remaining darkness he could feel surrounding him.

"Of course, master," the ancient warlord said, putting his sword in his scabbard at his waist.

He looked around at everyone. Myasako had never seen anything so heavily armored.

"But my duty is not yet done," Golhara said. "There is one more battle I must fight."

Battle

***A clear mind in battle allows
physical skill to be expressed.***

Chapter 15 - The Guardian

Quen had not worn his armour for many years. As he stepped out of his darkened room, his assistant heard the clinking of armour and stamps of metallic feet as he emerged, having to stoop his head down low so that he could make it out of the doorway.

He was taller than she thought he was. She had never seen him standing, up close, but now that he stood before her, with armoured hands that looked like claws and a large, jagged sword at his waist, she started to tremble slightly.

"Are you ready, sir? We have your vehicle arranged."

"Take me to the dogs," Quen said.

*

Quen's assistant, Hinoi, sat beside him in the back of an armoured vehicle. Quen didn't move. He didn't even look out of the window. None of his body was exposed to the air except for his eyes. Hinoi could see tinges of red within them when she dared to look at them for brief moments.

"Don't look at me anymore," Quen said. "I don't like it."

"Yes, sir," Hinoi said, and for the rest of the journey, she turned away and looked out of the window.

*

When they arrived at the underground compound, Quen and Hinoi could hear the ferocious snarling and barking of dogs through cages as their vehicle pulled up beside them. Hinoi froze. She felt such a fear within her, it was as if she was waking up within a nightmare, but she couldn't find her way out. She had never seen these dogs up close, either. She looked out of her window at them, and she could almost feel their intent biting through the armour-plated door. They wanted to kill her, they wanted to eat her and share her amongst themselves so that they could all benefit. Somehow they all felt like one unit, temporarily split into individual savages who only wanted blood.

Their fangs looked like they could cut through metal. Their eyes looked soulless. They almost looked hairless, just covered in skin, and their nostrils reminded Hinoi of underground train tunnels.

"Get out," Quen said.

Hinoi hesitated. She had always thought that her master had a valid reason to seek to take over the land. He had political reasons, social reasons, but now that she saw his operation up close, she could sense far more evil than she ever realised from speaking to Quen across a darkened room.

She slowly stepped out. There were ten cages before her, each with a dog inside. As Quen stepped out and walked around the vehicle, the dogs began to sniff furiously. Their sniffs sounded like heavy iron chains being dragged across the ground, and Quen walked and stood before them. The snarling and barking began to stop. Quen walked up and down the row of cages, allowing each dog to get a good sniff. One of the dogs kneeled, then another, then another, until all the dogs seemed to be almost bowing before Quen, ready to serve him.

"They are fantastic creatures," Quen said. "I would like to see one tested."

There were a team of three scientists standing off to the side.

"How so, sir?"

"Release one."

"Sir, that wouldn't be at all safe within such a confined area. At least if we release them in the woods, we will have space to..."

"Release one. Now," Quen said.

The guards surrounding them in the background all began to raise their rifles in anticipation. The scientists knew that at this stage, no weapon and no dart would be able to pierce through the dogs' skin. They were too far gone. These dogs had been bred to be indestructible.

"I will not ask again," Quen said. "Who is in charge? Who is the lead scientist here?"

"I am." A thin man named Fenshin stepped forward. He pushed his glasses up the rim of his nose as he stepped forward. They kept slipping down.

"Do it," Quen said. "They are clearly obedient to me."

Fenshin reached inside his pocket nervously. He looked at the other two scientists, who were beginning to back away.

"Now..." Quen said, as he watched Fenshin find the right key for the cage amongst the bundle in his shaking hands. "Do we have any spare prisoners? Any that we are not utilising in some way?"

The two scientists behind Fenshin nodded.

"Go and fetch one. A strong one, if possible. I want to see what one of these dogs can really do. And if it does what I've been told it can do, then I will be sure to reward you."

The two remaining scientists turned, beckoning three guards to accompany them as they walked out of a door into a brightly lit corridor, to go and find one of the prisoners that were being kept on the other side of the building.

*

After ten minutes, a large man in chains appeared at the same door, surrounded by three guards and followed by the two scientists. The lead scientist, Fenshin, was standing at the door of the nearest dog's cage, still shaking, ready to unlock it and let the mutant out.

As the prisoner was led through the door into this underground section of the compound, he looked at the dogs, then at Quen.

"So it's true," the prisoner said in a deep voice. "You've really gone and done it."

"Who is this?" Quen said.

Fenshin turned to Quen to explain.

"We found this one when we ventured into the woods to spy on the wolves. It was a few months ago. He ambushed us. We managed to sedate him and bring him here."

"You're lucky I hadn't eaten for months," the man said. "I'd barely drunk anything, either. My reserves had been dwindling."

Quen stared at the man. The man stared back. Considering the deprived conditions the prisoners were all kept in, he still looked huge and strong. Dirt covered his skin and brown shorts was all he had on. He was looking at Quen as if he wanted to fight him.

"And what is your name?" Quen said, taking a sudden interest in the apparent strength of this man.

"They call me the Guardian."

"And what do you do?"

"I protect things."

Quen paused and looked at Fenshin.

"Release the dog," Quen said.

"This won't be a contest," the man said, raising his chained hands so that Fenshin stopped and watched. "I won't put up a fight against that thing, not in these chains. And I've barely been fed. Give me one good meal, with fresh water and something grown from the Earth. Then I'll fight this thing and see if it's really up to the task I hear you want it to carry out. If it bites me once, I'm yours anyway, aren't I? You look like a former warrior yourself. Give me a fighting chance."

Quen did not like being called a *former* warrior. He *was* a warrior. It was in his blood.

"Or do you want the easy way out?" the Guardian said. "There are things far stronger than me in those woods, you know. You need to test it out properly first, don't ya?"

Quen stood and stared at the man. The Guardian was smiling slightly, testing Quen, questioning how strong his team of dogs really was.

Quen looked at the scientists.

"This is a strong one, sir, we've heard that if he has a good meal he is quite formidable. We don't advise that you..."

"Give him a full meal. Quickly," Quen said. "Let's see if he fights as well as his face says he can."

*

The Guardian was brought a large meal. Four plates of food and five glasses of water. He ate as if he was inhaling the food and drink, and Quen began to put his hand on the handle of his own sword as he noticed this large, dirty, muscled man was starting to grow just from eating a large meal.

The Guardian was still in chains. He finished the food quickly, licked the plates and stood up.

"Right!" he said. His voice was now booming. "I had not been fed like that in months! When I ambushed you lot I had just emerged from hibernation. You were lucky I was not in this kind of condition. Thank you for the meal. Now release the dog."

The Guardian stood to his feet, flipped over the table and plates, and he broke his chains off his own arms in one swift motion. A guard instinctively fired a dart at the Guardian's neck. The Guardian ducked, caught the dart in his own thick fingers, then threw the dart straight back at the guard's throat. The guard fell to the floor.

"Release that dog!" the Guardian yelled. Quen took out his sword. He was worried.

"I'll have you too, you armoured villain! I am the Guardian! No one can beat me one-on-one."

"Release the dog!" Quen shouted, and the scientist named Fenshin turned the key, and the giant dog suddenly launched itself at the Guardian.

The dog obeyed Quen's intent: to kill the Guardian, but as the massive dog snarled and barked and bared its fangs and leapt across the ground to land on the Guardian, the Guardian grabbed it by its front legs, turned his back and slammed the dog head-first into the ground. The concrete crumbled and cracked, and the dog's head was stuck inside the ground for a few seconds. The Guardian pulled it out of the ground by its rear legs and started to smash the dog into the ground, over and over again, head first, until the dog's thrashing and salivating and violent intent was nullified, and soon it was completely still, and unconscious.

"Bring me another one," the Guardian said, cracking his knuckles.

The guards raised their rifles.

"Stop," Quen said to all of them. "I will deal with him. Release the other dogs."

"Sir," Fenshin said, "sir that would be..."

"Release them," Quen said. "We have no more time to spare. They will be forming defences in the forest as we speak if Hinzen has shared my plans with them. The time to act is now. We cannot wait for these dogs to develop any further. If one of them bites this man, then he will be mine. Loyal to me. Release the dogs." Quen raised his sword.

"Oh, let's have it then!" the Guardian screamed, and he ran, bare-fisted and with eyes like venom, sprinting directly at Quen, as Fenshin scrambled around to quickly unlock all of the other cages. Soon nine dogs were being released, sprinting towards the Guardian, who was already standing in front of Quen, ducking under a slice from Quen's sword, wrapping his hand around Quen's armoured neck and snatching him to the ground.

All the guards began to back away as they watched. This Guardian was picking up dogs, throwing them into the ground, breaking their legs and kicking them across their faces. Four were already dealt with, and Quen was lying on the ground, struggling to stand up amongst the chaos of dogs and a ferocious Guardian.

But just for one moment, as Quen stood back up and grabbed at his sword, the Guardian turned, kicked Quen in the chest, and a dog's fang managed to scrape across the Guardian's back.

The Guardian kept fighting. He didn't feel it, and after the other five dogs were lying on the floor, broken and unconscious, the Guardian was on top of Quen.

The Guardian isolated one of Quen's arms, the arm with the sword, and he ripped the arm away from Quen's body.

Quen screamed as he felt his shoulder detach from his body, and he saw the Guardian raising the arm away, which still held Quen's sword in its hand.

"*My* arm," the Guardian said, "and now *your life* is mine..."

Quen had never seen such a ferocious fighting machine. He felt as if he were about to lose his life, as if he was about to vanish into nothing, but suddenly, the Guardian stood to his feet.

"It bit me. Something got me," the Guardian muttered, fighting to control his own limbs. He couldn't help but stand and step away from Quen.

He could feel something seeping in through his back, something cold that wanted to take control of his mind.

"You are mine," the Guardian grimaced. "No. No, you are mine, I'm about to end this, I'm about to take your life."

The Guardian dropped to one knee. Quen began to smile, despite having lost his arm.

"No," Quen said. "*You* are *mine*."

Master

Let your inner being be your primary master.

Chapter 16 - The Guardian's Master

Quen had been rushed to the medical room. He was being wheeled on a large bed. The Guardian's scratch from the tooth of a dog had now taken full effect over his mind.

"Master, master I'm sorry, what have I done?!" the Guardian said, walking heavily after the scientists who were wheeling Quen through the corridors. "Master, I didn't realise what I was doing. After my fight with the dogs, they made me see, master, they made me see how valuable you are, how it is only right to serve you and your intent."

"It's okay," Quen smiled. "I will soon be fixed."

"We have extra drugs, sir, extra things that will make you more powerful in battle," a scientist said.

"Good," Quen said, knowing that the searing pain in his shoulder would soon be fixed. The Guardian was carrying Quen's arm in both of his own, cradling it, with Quen's sword lying across the top.

"Never again, master, never again will I betray you. Are the dogs okay? I hurt them."

"They will be okay," Fenshin the scientist said. "They regenerate themselves quickly."

"Make sure you give the Guardian as much food and drink as he can possibly have, as much as he wants," Quen said as he stared up at the ceiling.

"Yes, sir," Fenshin said.

"Oh, thank you master, thank you. I feel such loyalty for you running through my veins."

"That was the plan," Quen said. "I can't wait to see you at work in the forest."

When Quen said the word 'forest', the Guardian stopped for a brief second. He had a feeling of being at home, a feeling of being safe and secure and loved. It made him stop following Quen on his bed, and it reminded him of a time where he felt free, free from any masters or methods of control.

Then he snapped out of it, and he continued to follow his new master, that for some reason, he felt as if he had known for years.

*

The Guardian watched as they operated on his master. There were all sorts of fluids and injection needles beside him on the bed.

"Will he be okay?" the Guardian said to Fenshin.

"Yes. Now, sir," Fenshin said, turning to Quen. "This is a novel drug we have been developing. It is not yet fully tested. Our fully tested one will grow back a limb in three days. This one can do it in three minutes, in most cases."

"Use this one. The quick one," Quen said. "We don't have any time to waste. Give me everything you can. Give the dogs everything extra that you can. They are clearly loyal to me. Pump them full of anything else you have." Fenshin nodded to the two other scientists, who scurried out of the room with a final dosing plan for the dogs. They had stumbled across an idea in the last few hours, to place something in the dogs' food that would make their bones even denser and their muscles even more explosive.

"Give it to me. I can feel them," Quen said. "I can feel them in the forest, preparing for us, gathering creatures and teamwork and protective forces. Hinzen has betrayed me. We must hurry, the battle is ours to lose. We still have the advantage. Give me everything."

"Sir, I should warn you that the extra power could..."

"Stop talking," Quen said. "Just do it. Just administer the dose."

Fenshin took a large syringe filled with pink fluid, and he drove it straight into the empty shoulder joint of Quen, who suddenly began to scream.

Thoughts

Sometimes the thoughts you think are yours,
are really just the voices of someone else.

Chapter 17 - Connection

The ancient warlord suddenly took a sharp breath in.

"I have access to things out here, in these woods," the warlord said. "I am a relative of Quen. He is a descendent of my master. I can sense something, pain in him. In his body, in his shoulder." The ancient warlord pointed to his own left shoulder with his armoured finger.

"And power," the warlord said, "he is assembling more power, even more power. He has captives. He will empower them to serve him. Lots of prisoners, more than he realises..."

"Well we can't worry about that," Nayla said quickly.

"He's right, though," Hinzen said. "Over the years Quen's teams have accumulated so many prisoners, that if they were to become bitten by the dogs, he would have an army. They would not only become more powerful, but also completely loyal to Quen's mission. I fear we might be overwhelmed. These wolves, this warlord, you three ninjas, and you, Queen Of The Wolves, you might be overpowered by what Quen could bring here."

As they all stood around, not sure what to do next, they heard a faint rumbling.

"What's that!" the ancient warlord said, drawing his sword. The wolves started to growl at the ground, Nayla took out her daggers. Myasako looked at Takashi, who also drew his sword, and his father, who was not moving at all.

"These are friends," Kuyasaki said. "Help is coming."

The shaking in the ground continued to grow larger, and soon, right in the middle of the group, up and out of the ground emerged Martin, wearing a shining green coat. The dirt began to shake itself off him, and out of the ground climbed his mother, Amanda, then the Garganfan, and then Jericho, the Coatmaker's grandson.

"These are friends," Kuyasaki said again, reassuring the wolves, who gradually calmed down.

As Kuyasaki looked at Martin, it was clear that he was developing into a different creature altogether.

"How you have grown," Kuyasaki said, bowing to Martin.

Martin bowed back, knowing that this meeting would soon happen. Kuyasaki stepped up to Martin and put his hand on Martin's shoulder.

"You are becoming a great warrior, a great caretaker of these forests," Kuyasaki said. "Your training with me was only the beginning, and there is far more for you to discover."

For the first time, Martin saw Kuyasaki smile, very slightly. There was suddenly a great warmth emerging out of him that Martin never knew was there.

"Martin," Myasako said, realising who it must have been when he saw Amanda stepping out of the ground. Myasako bowed to the both of them.

"Amanda," Myasako said, acknowledging her too.

"Thank you," Martin said, looking at Myasako and walking up to embrace him.

Martin opened his arms and hugged Myasako so tightly and with such a sense of power, Myasako was sure that if Martin wanted to, he could have crushed Myasako's spine.

But he didn't. He was gentle.

"Thank you for saving my mother when you were with her," Martin said. "Thank you for being so brave and skillful." Martin let go of Myasako, who bowed again.

"Of course, it was only right for me to help," Myasako said. "Thank you for coming to us, how did you get here?"

"It's a bit of a long story," Martin said. He turned to his accomplices. "This is my mother, of course. This is the Garganfan, and this is Jericho."

The Garganfan bowed to Kuyasaki and the ninjas. The wolves all recognised the Garganfan, and as they surrounded him, they bowed too.

"He helped us, too," Nayla said. "How can I remember all of this? I wasn't even born. It's like I'm viewing it through someone else's eyes. It was this creature, the Garganfan, and Kuyasaki's master, Hirozama, they helped us, hundreds of years ago. They stopped us from being enslaved. They fought against armoured men, men with armour like the warlord's, but it was dark and grim armour with a foul stench that we will always remember."

"I must confess," the ancient warlord said. "I was once your enemy. But I am now renewed, refreshed, clear, ready to serve what is right."

Amanda was very quiet. Myasako saw that she had changed. Her body looked different, stronger, and she looked completely connected to the Earth. Despite all of this strangeness around her, she looked content and peaceful. She waved at Myasako. Myasako waved back.

"We've heard about what's coming," Martin said. "We've heard about what Quen wants to do. We're ready to help. We're ready to serve."

"I just had an idea," Jericho said. "Do any of you remember a creature called the Strategist?"

Jericho looked around at everyone. The Garganfan was the only one who was nodding.

"Not many know of him," the Garganfan said. "He likes to take no credit and he stays out of sight of nearly everyone."

"He is here," Jericho said. "I saw him. I actually saw him, two weeks ago."

"On ground?" the Garganfan said.

"Yes! Yes on ground! I know it's not normal, but he had a notepad and pen, he was walking around, looking at the ground inspecting things. Sometimes he was on all fours, sniffing at the ground, getting his uniform dirty. I went to ask him what he was doing but he ordered me not to come closer. Once he was finished surveying something, he ran off up a tree and I haven't seen him since."

"How can you be sure he's still here?" Martin said. "And what do you want him to do?"

"He will help us bring all of this together," Jericho said. "He is a master at strategising battle! He's a true genius. I'm sure I could find him. There's a way, isn't there?"

The Garganfan nodded.

"Yes," the Garganfan said. "But it is not without risk."

"Only three of us should go," Jericho said. "He doesn't like dealing with more than three creatures at once. Garganfan, you know him so you should go. I think you should go, Martin, because of that coat of yours, and perhaps the ancient warlord should go since he has the empowered sword."

Jericho could see Golhara's sword still shining out of its scabbard. The ancient warlord turned to Kuyasaki.

"Master?"

Kuyasaki was silent for a moment.

"The master Kuyasaki is more worthy than me," Golhara said. "He knows more of strategy. The last strategy I had in battle was to attempt to rob my own master of his weapons and armour at the time. I am not worthy of such a meeting, not yet. I will stand guard here with the others. My master should go."

Jericho looked at Kuyasaki, who still wasn't saying anything.

"Very well," Jericho said. "Then Kuyasaki, perhaps you should go. I can show you where I think he might be, but you are the ones who must go to see him."

Kuyasaki stepped forward.

"Show us," he said.

Strategy

Let strategy be born from
clear focus on desired outcomes.

Chapter 18 - The Strategist

They did not need any underground root portals this time. Martin walked behind the Garganfan and marvelled at the forest around him. Kuyasaki walked behind him, and Jericho led the way. They were walking briskly, but Martin felt as if he was gliding.

"Here," Jericho said. They hadn't been walking for very long at all. Martin was almost certain that he could still smell the wolves.

"Up there," Jericho said. "Something told me it saw the Strategist climb up this tree, just yesterday."

Martin stared at the huge tree in front of them. It had a subtle tinge of green.

Martin instinctively began to speak to the tree.

"How can we find the Strategist?" Martin said.

The tree seemed to bow slightly in the presence of the Garganfan, and then Martin.

"Please answer the Tree Whisperer," the Garganfan said.

"I would, my lord..." the tree replied. Kuyasaki knew that something was going on, but he could not quite make out what the tree was saying. "But you see," the tree continued, "the Strategist swore me to secrecy. He made me promise that if he used me to hide away, then I would keep very quiet about his whereabouts. You know the rewards that come from a tree who holds home for a Strategist of any kind."

"What will happen if you tell us?" the Garganfan said.

"He will probably run off," the green-tinged tree said.

"We require his services," the Garganfan said. "There is a war coming, a battle for this forest is soon to take place, and we are looking to defend it. We ask for the Strategist's help."

Martin noticed that Jericho had edged away, out of sight.

"Here," they heard a little voice say.

They all turned around. Kuyasaki had never allowed himself to be snuck up on so easily. All three turned around, and could see nothing.

"Here," the voice came to their left. They turned. All they could see was trees.

"Here," the voice said again, and standing in front of the large, green-tinged tree, stood a little brown creature dressed in a small green military uniform. To Martin it looked a bit like a badger, but with dark brown fur and a much longer snout.

"I know they are coming," the Strategist said. "You need not explain that to me."

"We ask for your help," the Garganfan said, dropping to one knee. Martin and Kuyasaki copied.

"Do you know what happened the last time you asked me for help?" the Strategist said, beginning to pace up and down in front of the three kneeling figures.

"Yes," the Garganfan said.

"You lost your place as the King Of The Trees. I failed to deliver a plan that kept you safe and in your rightful place."

"It was my own fault," the Garganfan said, looking up. "Your plan was as good as it could have been."

"I have carried great guilt within me from that time," the Strategist said, looking up at the trees all around him, "only to realise that the guilt began to eat away at my life force. I nearly gave up, you know. I nearly went back into the Earth."

"We are glad you are still here. We need help arranging our forces."

"You need more recruits, too," the Strategist said, beginning to pace up and down again. His voice reminded Martin of an old war hero he had seen on the TV once. He was cutting and blunt with his words, but he always wanted to do the best he could for the things he cared about.

"More recruits?" the Garganfan said. "We have assembled some powerful..."

"It's not enough!" the Strategist snapped. "They have taken a Guardian!"

The Garganfan stood to his feet. Martin and Kuyasaki did the same.

"A Guardian?" the Garganfan said. "I heard murmurs amongst the trees, I wasn't sure if..."

"It's true," the Strategist said. "If they have managed to turn him, then may Nature help us all. They don't just have a Guardian, you know. They have taken other things. They have taken Fengmoths, Albursitches, Hennonflies, even Wallmasters, they even took a Qualsatcher!"

"How? When?" the Garganfan said. He looked around at the trees. They were letting the Strategist speak.

"Over the course of the past few months. They have been doing it very gradually, so as not to provoke a strong response from the forest. Little by little they have been invading, checking, researching, capturing.

"I have even seen one of the dogs," the Strategist said, looking at Kuyasaki. "You. It was you, wasn't it? You rode it into the forest and killed it with your own hands."

Kuyasaki nodded.

"They are stronger now, I expect," the Strategist said. "Much stronger. There was something manic in that dog, some kind of manic, destructive trait destined to grow larger and larger until it grows indestructible. I have had spies at work, little Menonflies have been reporting to me that the dogs are at least twice as powerful as when this large ninja dealt with one. There are lots of them. At least forty."

Martin heard a very slight buzzing. A little green fly flew past his head and landed on the Strategist's shoulder. It began to buzz more loudly.

"Good grief," the Strategist said. "They have turned the Guardian over to their side. And they are coming with an army."

*

"I have been making detailed notes recently," the Strategist said, after listening to all that the little fly had to say. "For some reason I found myself

143

surveying the area, making notes of terrain and latent powers held within each section of the forest. It changes over time. Then I heard of Quen's scientists beginning to enter into these woods, and I knew that a plan of action would soon be necessary."

Martin could sense that Jericho was hiding somewhere behind them, somewhere behind the cover of a large tree.

"Tell that Coatmaker's descendent that he may emerge," the Strategist said. "It is a myth that I can only ever meet with three creatures."

Jericho heard what was said, and he began to walk towards the group.

"But I can not handle large numbers!" the Strategist quickly said. "You four will suffice. I will draw you up a plan. My spies have told me the angles that they plan to attack from. With the right recruits we will be ready. What forces have you accumulated already?"

Martin listed the number of wolves he had seen, Takashi, Myasako...

"Then there is Nayla," Kuyasaki said. "You are yet to meet her properly, Martin. She is a powerful one."

"What else? Who else?" the Strategist said.

"The ancient warlord named Golhara," Kuyasaki said. "He seeks to serve us in protecting the forest."

"Good, good, but it's not enough, as I suspected," said the Strategist, rubbing his chin with his fingers. "Go back to your group, except you, Garganfan. You will stay with me. As King Of The Trees, you can help me warn and recruit every helpful creature in this forest, and once we see who is willing to help, I can draw up a plan of action. Go now, you three, go!"

Martin, Kuyasaki and Jericho turned and began to walk back towards Nayla, the wolves, Hinzen and the ancient warlord.

Martin looked at the Garganfan for reassurance. The Garganfan nodded.

"I will see you soon," the Garganfan said, and as Martin continued to walk away, he looked back and saw the Garganfan suddenly in the distance, disappearing amongst the trees, carrying the Strategist on his shoulder.

Team

The formation of a team allows
for maximum output of strength.

Chapter 19 - The Great Meeting

"That's it! That's it!" the Strategist was saying, riding on the shoulder of the sprinting Garganfan. It almost felt as if the Garganfan had found a direct path, a direct straight line to travel through the trees to get to the sacred meeting point, a space in the forest that he could remember from his past.

"Amazing!" the Strategist said. "The King Of The Trees has returned!"

It was almost as if the trees were parting ways for him as he ran, everything cleared in the presence of the Garganfan, and now that he was once again reunited with the Strategist, in the same forest where he had once fought his most testing war, the Garganfan was beginning to feel his rightful place in the forest.

"The King Of The Trees!" he heard the trees around him begin to shout. "The King Of The Trees has regained his true place! His heart has returned!"

The Garganfan knew exactly where to go.

"You still remember where it is, don't you?" the Strategist said. "We need to move quickly."

Another green buzzing Menonfly managed to catch up to them and land on the Strategist's shoulder.

The Strategist listened to what the Menonfly had to say.

"They are preparing to leave soon. Quen and his army, they are on their final doses of power-enhancing drugs! I will prepare my speech."

As the Garganfan continued to leap and sprint through the forest, the Strategist was somehow managing to balance on top of his shoulder using one hand to hold his notepad, and the other to write a speech that he would need to rally as many creatures in the forest as he possibly could.

*

"Master," the Guardian bowed as Quen stood up after ten minutes of agonising screaming. Quen's arm had grown back, and his body was larger than before. He stood beside his bed in the operating room.

"This is truly amazing," Quen said. "I feel...I feel a new life within me."

"We still can't be sure of the side effects, sir," Fenshin the scientist said as he arranged his remaining vials and syringes neatly by the bed.

"How many prisoners do we have left?" Quen said, realising what great power he now had with the Guardian by his side.

"We currently have one hundred and fifty, sir."

Quen stopped thinking and turned to look down on Fenshin. Fenshin started to tremble. He was regretting injecting Quen with such a strong dose of drug, when he saw the new look in Quen's eyes.

Quen took one step forward, wrapped his now bare, unarmoured new hand around Fenshin's throat, and lifted Fenshin up into the air, so that his feet were dangling and Fenshin was choking.

"Why didn't you tell me this before? This is very important. That is more than I expected," Quen said, waiting for a response.

Fenshin was struggling to breathe.

Quen released Fenshin and he fell to the ground, gasping for breath.

"This armour is now too small for me," Quen said. "You have made me grow out of it, Fenshin! You never warned me!"

Quen started to rip the armour off the rest of his body, and he began to feel as if he was being born again, removing all the limitations of his past and finally being free to move as he wanted.

Fenshin struggled to stand up.

"You probably won't need armour now, sir."

"What?" Quen said.

"The drug, the power of it. It likely made you impenetrable, especially when mixed with your warlord heritage."

"Test it," Quen said, turning to the Guardian who was still holding Quen's old arm, covered in armour that he had ripped from the socket when his mind was free and rebellious.

"How, master?" the Guardian said.

"Use my sword," Quen said, taking it out of its scabbard and handing it to the Guardian.

"Cut me," Quen said.

"No, master, I can't, I..."

"Do it! I'm ordering you," Quen snapped.

The Guardian nodded, and he reluctantly thrust the tip of the sword into Quen's stomach.

"Harder," Quen said. "Pierce through the body."

The Guardian drove the tip of the sword forcefully into Quen's stomach. Nothing happened, the sword seemed to bounce off.

"Again," Quen said.

Soon the Guardian was stabbing and thrashing and slicing at Quen's body, and the sword kept bouncing off and flying back in the direction it had been thrust in. Quen was beginning to smile.

"I'm impenetrable," Quen said. "You have done it, Fenshin. You have made me indestructible."

"The side effects though, sir, we aren't sure if..."

"How much of this stuff do you have?" Quen said.

"Lots," Fenshin said. "Lots in storage. It's easy to make, we simply..."

"Can you give it to all of the prisoners?"

"Yes sir, but their loyalty must first be shifted. They need to be bitten by the dogs."

"We will set the dogs on them then. I will tell them only to bite, not to kill or badly injure. Then we will give the prisoners what you just gave me, and the army we will have assembled..."

Quen started to shake with the thought of all the power that would be at his fingertips.

"Along with our forty dogs – give them that too," Quen said, pointing to the empty syringe by the side of the bed. "Give everything a dose of this stuff."

"Sir," Fenshin said, "that might be too much for the dogs, we can't predict what..."

"Do it!" Quen snapped. "And give the Guardian here a dose of it too. Act quickly, Fenshin! We will be leaving soon. Time is of the essence. Hurry!"

"Yes sir," Fenshin said, beginning to prepare a dose for the Guardian.

"Our time is now," Quen said, smiling at the Guardian. The Guardian bowed and presented Quen's sword back to him.

"Yes, master," the Guardian said, and as Quen took his sword back, the Guardian had a brief but intense thought of himself in the forest, fighting, ripping and tearing creatures apart. But in that short and confusing flash in his mind, he was not fighting against other creatures in the forest. He was fighting against the dogs.

*

When the Garganfan and the Strategist arrived in the sacred meeting space, the Strategist jumped off the Garganfan's shoulder and began to look around.

The Garganfan was not at all out of breath.

"Hear me!" the Strategist called out. He began to look at his speech on his notepad. Then he put the notepad in his pocket, deciding that he would speak spontaneously.

"A great battle is coming!" the Strategist called. "Creatures, strange and empowered creatures, many of which would have once served to protect this forest, have been turned against us and wish to serve the evil intent of a warlord named Quen! We need your help, all who can hear me! If we do not fight against these invaders, they will have a chance at taking over the purity of this forest and ruling it for their own ends! We must fight back! We must stand and fight and protect the sanctity of these woods.

"There was once a battle like this, hundreds of years ago, where there was an attempt to capture and enslave the inhabitants of this forest. And now the time has come again to rally together and defend our borders from those who try to ruin what is so sacred. The King Of The Trees has returned. We ask that you help us!"

The Garganfan looked around. He could sense that creatures everywhere were watching and listening, but he could not see any of them.

The Strategist looked around.

"Where is your weapon?" the Strategist said.

"What weapon?" the Garganfan said.

153

"Do you not remember?" the Strategist said. "You used to have a staff. It was made of wood and roots from other fallen Garganfans. You used to use it in battle, it gave you powers so strong that..."

The Garganfan suddenly remembered things from his past that he had not thought about for hundreds of years. He thought of all the damage he had done...

"I gave it up," the Garganfan said. "When I realised all the blood that had been shed at my own hands, when I realised that my power was too much for me to handle, I gave up my staff shortly after I sacrificed my heart." The Garganfan touched the gleaming stone in his chest. "And without my heart, it was never much use to me, anyway."

"What did you do with it?" the Strategist said. "You know that you cannot wield your full power over the forest without your heart *and* your staff."

"I...I just dropped it," the Garganfan said. "When I gave up and fell back into the Earth, I just dropped it."

"Well command it! Get it back!" the Strategist said. "It's vital. I thought you had it stored somewhere, not that you just let it go!"

"I was too powerful," the Garganfan said, "my temper was so strong that..."

"You need it," a little voice said. It was a small mousy creature that walked out from behind a tree. "We are nothing without your staff and your heart," the little mousy creature said.

"Mousann? Is that you?" the Garganfan said.

The little mouse standing on its hind legs nodded, and walked up to the Garganfan. The Garganfan kneeled and embraced Mousann.

"You look different," the Garganfan said.

"Smaller, I know," Mousann said. "When you gave up your powers, it took many of ours away with it, too. The amount of creatures willing to fight for the forest are less now. They feel disempowered. Ever since the King Of The Trees fled from his own kingdom, from his own throne, so many creatures have lost confidence and power. The Guardian on the western border even had to start hibernating. Your staff is not just for you. It's for all of us."

The Garganfan stood and looked down at the little creature who he could remember being so formidable in battle.

"What if it happens again?" the Garganfan said. "What if I become corrupted?"

"You have evolved," the Strategist said. "You were never in communion with your heart as you could be now. The Garganfan I knew would have already stormed into Quen's compound and recklessly slaughtered anything that stood in its way. You are wiser now. Your heart is brighter."

The little creature named Mousann had whiskers that were twitching.

"But you have to merge with it," Mousann said, quietly. "You have to merge with the wisdom of your heart so that you don't become stuck in your head again. You have to let the power of your heart take over your entire mind so that you can be a tool for its energy."

The Garganfan's attention fell fully into his own heart from a moment, and out of the ground in front of him, with a slight rumble of the Earth, emerged a wooden staff wrapped and covered in hardened, dark tree roots.

"Yes!" Mousann said. "That's it. No more thinking for yourself. Let your heart do it all for you. There's so much intelligence there, we all know it! We've all known it except for you."

The Garganfan had switched off his mind, his struggle with his past, his regret and guilt and conflict with who he was. It was silent within him. The stone in his chest was reaching through every cell of his woody body, and he knelt down to pick up his staff.

"And now," the Strategist said, "the war is ours to win."

The Garganfan touched the staff, and everything around him seemed to explode. He re-lived every moment he had ever lived, re-fought every battle he had ever fought, until he surrendered to it all, stopped fighting against what had happened, and now stood in the eternal present, where everything was golden and powerful.

Creatures began to emerge from behind the trees. Mousann's body began to grow and his teeth began to turn into fangs.

There were gorilla-like creatures beginning to swing down from the trees. There were powerful deer with antlers that looked like they were made of stone. There were rodents like Mousann beginning to shift and grow and become more muscular. And then, from far up in the trees, they could all see the branches beginning to move.

"They have been waiting for you," the Strategist said, watching more woody creatures begin to drop and fly down to the Earth, only to stand and bow at their lord and king.

"The Garganfans have been waiting," the Strategist said.

157

Evolution

Life is a process of evolution,
within each and every body.

Chapter 20 - The Final Test

As Kuyasaki, Martin and Jericho walked back towards Myasako, Nayla, Takashi, Hinzen and the wolves, Kuyasaki began to test Martin.

"Show me your skills," Kuyasaki said.

Martin noticed that Kuyasaki had stopped walking.

"How?" Martin said. "Do you want to spar?"

"Yes."

Jericho took a few steps back.

"I think with the coat on, it might be unfair," Martin said. He didn't mean for it to sound so arrogant, but he knew that the coat he was wearing had unbelievable powers that made him feel almost inhuman.

"The coat you are wearing merely channels the Earth's energies through you," Kuyasaki said. "One day you will not need that coat. It helps you receive power to a greater extent. If you are to use it in battle today, you should leave it on. I want to see how capable you are before Quen and his army arrive."

"Okay," Martin said, taking a deep breath in. He had a quick memory of being in Kuyasaki's dojo in

Japan, when his body was weak and his mind was always distracted.

"Don't hold back," Kuyasaki said. "Go!"

Kuyasaki did not draw his weapons, but he ran at Martin so quickly that Martin was suddenly ducking under a kick. He didn't realise Kuyasaki could move this fast. He realised that for all the time he had spent with him in the dojo, Kuyasaki was always holding back.

Soon Kuyasaki was on top of Martin again, and even with the coat, Martin was struggling to keep up.

Martin instinctively raised his arm to grab and protect his own head, and Kuyasaki landed a punch on his arm. Kuyasaki was not throwing the punch hard, but it was so fast that soon Kuyasaki was touching Martin's stomach, then his knee, then his head again when Martin was distracted.

"You aren't using the coat enough," Kuyasaki said. "You must take advantage of everything that is available to you. You seem to still think that using the coat would be cheating."

Martin wondered how Kuyasaki knew this. Martin hadn't even realised it himself.

"Use it," Kuyasaki said. "It has come to you. We must all use the powers available to us. Use the coat."

Soon Kuyasaki had darted to the left of Martin and was kicking at his head again. Martin blocked it and stumbled back. He felt overwhelmed. He actually felt disheartened.

"Why do you not use the coat?" Kuyasaki snapped, rushing towards Martin and grabbing at Martin's head and wrapping his arm around Martin's neck.

Martin's head was soon stuck in Kuyasaki's armpit. With all the physical strength he thought he had developed over recent times, he still couldn't budge Kuyasaki. It was like being held in a gentle but immovable vice.

"I will not let you go until you let that coat flow through you," Kuyasaki said. "Be a vehicle for it."

Martin stopped struggling so much. He took a breath. He stopped fighting against himself and Kuyasaki's immense speed and strength. He could feel the coat's energy trying to flow into his body.

"What do you want to do?" Martin said.

He asked the question, waited for an answer, and suddenly Kuyasaki was being lifted off his feet as Martin lifted him up into the air.

"Very good!" Kuyasaki said. "Yes, allow the coat to do what it wants. The Earthcoat always knows what is best."

Martin shrugged and slipped his head out of Kuyasaki's grip, and Kuyasaki gracefully landed on the ground, one foot after the other, and before Martin could think again and separate himself from the mind of the coat, Kuyasaki was once again on him, throwing strikes so quickly that Martin could barely see them.

Instead of cowering and trying to defend, Martin found himself slipping out the way of punches and firing his own punches back.

He nearly landed one.

"Much better," Kuyasaki said. "No one expects to have their attack thrown back at them while they are in the middle of their own. The coat knows best."

Kuyasaki edged towards Martin. This time Martin faked a punch to Kuyasaki's head and went to kick at him low. Kuyasaki jumped over the kick and pretended to stomp down on Martin's trailing leg which Martin managed to snap back quickly, and then Martin attacked again, kicking this time with such speed that he didn't know how he was doing it.

"Yes! Yes!" Kuyasaki said, "Now really let go."

As Kuyasaki backed up, then shifted to the side, he went to kick at Martin once more. Martin rolled, felt himself plant directly into the ground, and then an immense surge of energy came shooting up through the Earth, into Martin's legs and then through his body, until he was pointing at Kuyasaki, with a golden, fiery light shining out of his fingertips which engulfed Kuyasaki and held him frozen in place.

"You are ready," Kuyasaki said, suspended in the air. "You are now one with the Earthcoat."

Connection

Find oneness with your true power
by no longer fighting against it.

Chapter 21 - The Assembly

When Martin, Kuyasaki and Jericho arrived back at the others, the wolves were pacing around. Martin had the time to really look at them now. They all knew that a fight was soon upon them. They were becoming agitated and aggressive.

"We are ready," Nayla said to Kuyasaki. She looked at Martin, and Martin looked back.

"How did it go?" she said.

"Very well," Kuyasaki said. "The Garganfan and the Strategist went to recruit more creatures."

"Did he draw up a plan?"

"No yet," Kuyasaki said, "but he will do soon."

Martin heard whispers coming from the trees.

"The King Of The Trees has reclaimed his staff! The King Of The Trees has regained his throne!"

"The trees are saying the Garganfan has reclaimed his staff," Martin said.

"Good," Nayla said. "He needs it for full power."

"How do you know all of this?" Martin said to Nayla, gradually walking through the pack of pacing wolves. "You look no older than me."

"I feel old," Nayla said. "I feel as if I've lived through hundreds of years in different bodies now. I feel that once, I was a Queen, Queen Of The Wolves. Hinzen called me by that name earlier, and suddenly I remembered pieces of my past that at first I thought were just my imagination."

She looked at the ground for a moment.

"I'm Martin," Martin said. A handshake seemed too formal. He placed his hand on his heart.

"I'm Nayla," Nayla said. She placed her hand on her heart too.

Suddenly everyone felt the ground rumbling. There were chants, calls, noises, roars, shrieks, flapping of wings, every noise that one could imagine was flooding through the forest towards the group.

Myasako saw that Takashi drew his sword.

In the distance, Martin could see the Garganfan running towards them all, and he was being followed by a hoard of creatures. There were birds, giant rodents, strange colourful apes, huge antlered deer. And Martin was sure that far behind, he could see some bears.

The Garganfan was carrying a long staff covered in hard dark roots, and soon, with the Strategist on his shoulder, they were meeting with the group.

All the wolves stopped and began to sniff at the air, sniffing the scent of every creature that made its way towards them.

The hoard of creatures all gathered in front of the group, and the Garganfan stepped forward.

"Luckily, the Strategist has overcome his fear of large numbers," the Garganfan said, smiling slightly.

The Strategist jumped off the Garganfan's shoulder and pulled out a small, dark, folded-up piece of paper.

"It is necessary to step out of one's comfort zone from time to time!" the Strategist shouted, unfolding the small piece of paper into a large diagram that was almost the size of one of the great dark wolves.

"Now, here is the plan!" the Strategist said. "My flying insect informants have told me where they will be entering. It is unlikely that they will wait until nightfall. If they do, I am also told the dogs have been engineered with excellent night vision. But we can not be certain of this yet!

"This diagram shows all possible entry points," the Strategist continued. Martin looked at the diagram along with all of the other people and creatures that had gathered around the Strategist.

"The ninjas must stay together!" the Strategist said. "And by 'the ninjas', I mean you three," he said, pointing at Kuyasaki, Takashi, and Myasako. "You other two young ones have ninja within you, but you will be needed elsewhere. The three ninjas will remain here with the ancient warlord. You will fight off any intruders with the help of the great bears."

Two large, enormously tall bears waded through the crowd and sat beside the three ninjas.

"Those bears take no prisoners," the Strategist said. "And they can hear your thoughts."

Martin and Myasako were both sure that they had read about similar bears, but the bears they had read about wore great sets of armour and wielded swords that were passed down through their ancestors.

"Shouldn't they have armour?" Martin interrupted. The Strategist glared at him. His nose started to twitch.

"No questions yet!" the Strategist said. "But no. You are referring to the bears of the north. They died out a number of years ago. These are bears from the east. They don't need armour. It only slows them down."

"Okay, sorry," Martin said.

"You, young man!" the Strategist said, pointing at Martin. "You and your mother will head to this entrance."

The Strategist pointed to an area on the right of the diagram where the trees were not so dense.

"They are likely to attack from this point, too," the Strategist said. "You will be accompanied by the Garganfan, his team, and nothing more."

"Okay," Martin said. "What team?"

"Girl!" the Strategist said.

Nayla stepped forward. When the Strategist saw her, he kneeled.

"I apologise," he said, remorsefully. "Queen Of The Wolves. I see what they mean now. It is true. You are the Queen, reborn again in this forest. You are to head here." The Strategist pointed to an entrance to the forest on the far left of the diagram.

"You will go here with your wolves, accompanied by the Ferahawk birds." Nayla looked up in the trees and saw some of the grey, stone-like birds start to flap their wings and bob their heads up and down.

"Questions?" the Strategist asked. No one said anything.

"And finally, all of you who remain," the Strategist said. "You will all follow me, deeper into the woods. You will aid these three groups using methods formally unknown to many creatures in the forest. Follow me," the Strategist said, beginning to walk off deeper into the woods.

"Darkness is falling," the Strategist called back to the main group behind him. "Go to your battle stations. Those are the three areas where there is space in the trees for such large dogs to enter. May the forest be with you."

The Strategist jumped on the back of a large, heavily fanged rodent, and he rode off into the distance, with all the other animals and creatures except the birds and the bears, following after him.

The Garganfan turned to Martin. Now with his staff, he really looked like a king in Martin's eyes.

"Let's go," the Garganfan said.

King

Great leaders are those
who serve the ones they lead.

Chapter 22 - The Advance

Quen and the Guardian were sitting in the back of a large armoured vehicle. Quen was showing the Guardian a map. There was a Menonfly inside the vehicle, buzzing around, and it was starting to annoy Quen as it flew in front of his eyes, almost as if it was looking at the map as he was speaking.

"Who let that fly in?" Quen said. "Anyway, Guardian, these are the three entry points that we will be attacking from. All the dogs and prisoners are now loaded up in the trucks behind us, and we should be at the forest in approximately twenty minutes."

The Guardian looked at the map. Memories were trying to burst into his mind, memories about the forest, but something was stopping them.

"And where will we be going?" the Guardian said.

"Here," Quen said, pointing to the map on the furthest away entry point. "Here is where we will go with the dogs. We will flank the area where the wolves are said to dwell. Two other sets of prisoners and our guards will be at the other entry points."

"Hmm," the Guardian said. "Are you sure they'll be able to obey you if you are that far away?"

"Yes," Quen said, "the scientists have reassured me that as long as I am within a certain distance of the newly dosed prisoners, they will not be difficult to influence. It is the dogs that I have to stay close to, since they are so well-developed at this stage."

The Guardian nodded. He looked up at the fly that was now resting on the wall.

"There's something about that fly that I'm not sure I like," the Guardian said.

"What do you mean?" Quen said.

"I feel like it's watching us," the Guardian said.

Quen turned and looked up at the fly that remained motionless on the wall.

"What kind of fly is it?" Quen said.

"I don't know," the Guardian said, "a Mmm...a Mumfly, is it? I feel like I should be able to remember. The name's in me somewhere, but I can't quite find it."

Quen saw that the Guardian was trying to access his memories of what it was like to live in the forest, to be one with the forest, ready to fight off anything that came close to threaten it.

"Well, never mind that," Quen said. "Never mind the fly. It cannot escape from here, anyway. Just ready yourself. This will be the greatest battle you've ever fought. If the prisoners or the dogs, or even you, manage to bite into *anything* in that forest, then soon that creature will become loyal to me and my mission. We will be able to expand our army, and take it across towns and cities to ensure that the rightful will is done."

"And what's the rightful will?" the Guardian said.

Quen didn't like the tone. It sounded slightly less obedient as they were drawing closer to the forest.

"My will," Quen snapped. "My will. Once I take over this entire land, things will be done properly. Everyone will work in service to me, not to themselves and their own petty desires."

"Hmm," the Guardian nodded.

Quen leaned forward towards the Guardian. The Guardian felt Quen's anger surging through his own body.

"Are you ready?" Quen said. "Are you ready to capture and bite anything you can?"

"Yes, master," the Guardian said.

"The dogs will flood through the forest. Once they are inside, they will have freedom to sniff out and go after those wolves. The wolves are our priority, everything else that gets in the way will be more than welcome."

"Yes, master," and as the Guardian watched the fly on the wall of the armoured vehicle shake its wings slightly, he thought it was far better, for some reason, to just leave it alone.

Instinct

*Do not let the voices of others
override your true instincts.*

Chapter 23 - The Arrival

When the Guardian and Quen arrived at the edge of the forest, they climbed out of the back of the armoured vehicle and looked around. The Guardian noticed the little fly zoom past their heads and fly straight into the forest, disappearing as if it was on a mission.

The Guardian said nothing. Something about this place felt so homely. It was as if he was back with his mother, the mother he had been made to forget about.

Behind them the Guardian could see two lorries approaching. They were huge lorries, tall and black and long, and the Guardian could hear the snarling and barking and savagery rumbling out of the walls of the lorries as they approached.

"They are ready," Quen said.

Accompanied by guards on all sides of him, Quen walked around to the back of the first lorry.

The Guardian followed behind, but he kept looking into the trees.

"Open the door," Quen said to one of his guards. These were his finest guards, tall and strong and heavily armed, and one of them stepped forward and opened the back of the lorry so that the door went shooting up, contracting to the top.

The Guardian actually flinched. They looked far more evil now. The dogs were standing there, salivating, with eyes that looked like devils, with teeth so large, their top fangs almost reached the bottom of their chins.

"Step in, you six," he said to his guards.

"Sir?" one of the guards said.

"They won't hurt you," Quen said. "Let them sniff your hand. It's so they know you are safe. Take your gloves off first."

The first guard was hesitant, but was so used to doing as he was told, and knowing that Quen could easily set the dogs on him if he disobeyed, the large guard climbed up into the lorry-load of dogs, who were all standing, staring at him and beginning to snarl. The guard offered his hand. It was shaking slightly, and as one of the dogs went to sniff, it lightly pierced the guard's skin with one of its fangs.

"Did that hurt?" Quen said.

"No," the guard said. "Actually it felt quite pleasant."

"It gives you their strength. You will be needing it," Quen said.

"You, you all do the same," Quen said to the other guards, removing his sword from his waist and beckoning the guards to climb up into the lorry.

They did, and one by one, their hands were gently pierced, so that just a drop of blood oozed out.

"What's happening, sir?" the first guard said with a gasp, clutching at his own stomach.

"It's necessary," Quen said. "I didn't allow you to see what we did to the other prisoners, because I had the same thing planned for you."

The Guardian felt something in the air. He had a flashing thought of apes arise in his mind.

He watched as each of the strong guards kneeled and began to scream. They started to grow and swell and the sleeves of their uniforms began to tear apart at the seams. There were new muscles growing out of their necks and legs and shoulders, and they were expanding as they knelt there.

"What is this?!" the guard yelled.

"It's loyalty," Quen said, and as the guards started to morph into giant versions of themselves, the Guardian saw that they began to grab at the weapons at their waists.

"We serve you, and only you, master," they began to say in unison. "You are the master of everything.

We will capture and bite and influence anything that comes across our path. Our weapons will help us too."

Suddenly everything went dark for the Guardian. Something had landed on his back and was wrapping its dry, leathery palms around his eyes.

He was sure he could hear a few grunts and noises, and as he reached up to grab at the hands around his eyes, and the short hairy legs wrapped around his neck, he was picked up off the ground by another pair of hands and slammed into the road beneath him.

Even with all of his strength, he couldn't move. He was pinned to the ground.

"Release us, it's an ambush!" Quen said.

Then suddenly the Guardian heard the dogs barking, but at the same time heard the lorry door being slammed shut again.

A dog had escaped. The Guardian could hear it outside the lorry. Then the Guardian heard shrieks of monkeys and apes and gorillas that seemed so familiar to him, but he couldn't quite picture them in his mind.

Something above him shrieked, he was struck over the head, and for a while, it felt as if he was asleep.

Ambush

Remain aware of your surroundings,
without carrying fear in your mind.

Chapter 24 - The Ambush

When the Guardian woke up, he looked up at the trees and smiled. He was in the forest. For a moment he forgot all about his master Quen and what his mission was to carry out in the forest, and before he remembered, he sat up, and he looked around at thirty apes of all different shapes and colours, hanging from branches and sitting on the floor.

There was one of Quen's dogs lying beside them on the floor. It looked dead.

The Guardian noticed the dog started to stir.

One of the apes swung down from the trees and shoved its fists in the dog's nostrils. Two other apes, two large gorilla-looking creatures waddled over and clamped the dog's mouth shut.

"That's one of Quen's dogs," the Guardian muttered.

He looked around again as the apes were suffocating the dog that seemed to refuse to die.

"They are hard to kill," the Guardian said, rubbing his head. He felt confused.

"I'm supposed to serve Quen," the Guardian said, "aren't I? Or am I supposed to serve..."

Suddenly the Earth seemed to grip him from beneath, and he remembered his entire life. He remembered his birth, his parents, his battles, his duties, his inborn desire to protect the forest, and then he remembered being scratched across the back by one of the those dogs, then dosed with drugs in Quen's labs, and he started to shake off all the old loyalty that had been chemically injected into him.

"I'm no slave!" the Guardian said. The apes' eyes all widened, and they seemed to begin to smile. The Guardian saw that some of them were holding the weapons that the guards had been holding. But the Guardian could not see Quen's sword.

One of the apes nearby, a small brown monkey, beckoned the Guardian to climb a tree with him.

The Guardian obliged, gliding up the tree as easily as one of these great apes, and soon he was beside this small monkey, looking at the road in the distance with the two tall, black lorries.

"We disarmed them," the monkey said. The language of the monkeys was short and chirping, sometimes grunting, and the Guardian understood it perfectly.

"They will come again soon," the Guardian said. "Where are the wolves?"

The monkey pointed behind it.

"Further in," the monkey said. "Waiting."

"You can not risk being bitten by any of them!" the Guardian said. "If they bite you..."

"We know," the monkey said, "we have been warned. But we have a good strategy."

The Guardian heard something else climbing up the tree beneath them. It was a badgery-looking creature wearing a military uniform, holding a diagram in his hands. He was balancing on top of the shoulders of a dark gorilla.

"Good to have you back," the Strategist said. The Guardian recognised him instantly.

"It will be minutes before they enter," the Strategist said. "Quen will become far too angry to reconsider all of this. Here's the plan..."

*

When Quen woke up, his head was sore.

"Oh," he said, grabbing his head and climbing to his feet. His sword was in his hand, almost as if it was glued there. He couldn't let it go.

"Fenshin!" Quen called. He saw that the back of the lorry was now shut again, and his large, now unarmed guards were also staggering to their feet.

Fenshin jumped out of the front of the armoured vehicle. He had been in the passenger's seat, wanting to avoid the dogs at all costs.

"Yes, sir?" Fenshin said, running towards his master, still wearing a lab coat and holding a clipboard.

"What happened?" Quen said.

"The apes, sir. The great apes. I didn't see them coming either, sir, I didn't know they knew..."

"Well how could they have known we would be here? It was almost as if they knew beforehand..."

Fenshin looked at the ground.

"And what about our powers? You've injected me, the guards have been bitten, the Guardian was bitten *and* he was given an extra injection! How could we have been so easily beaten like that?"

Fenshin did not dare to look up.

"Answer me!" Quen shouted.

The lorry behind Fenshin started to rumble with angry dogs. They were trying to break through the reinforced walls.

"Sir...the great apes, they are known for their abominable strength. Strength like that is hard to replicate in the lab. That's why we are here, sir, to have them bitten, to make their strength our own."

Quen didn't know whether or not to strike Fenshin down where he stood.

Fenshin was still holding something back.

"What is it?" Quen said. "You better tell me or I'll..."

"They took the Guardian, sir. And I saw them dragging an unconscious dog into the forest, too."

Quen raised his sword.

"And they took my guards' weapons," Quen said quietly. Fenshin closed his eyes.

"Why not my sword?" Quen said, looking at it.

"I don't know, sir, perhaps your grip was too strong? Perhaps they were preoccupied with the one dog..."

Quen gently brought the edge of his blade to Fenshin's throat.

"And do you know what the worst part is?" Quen said, almost smiling at the thought of what he was soon going to do.

"No, sir."

"They might have managed to turn the Guardian back to their side. I could sense it, even during the journey here. His allegiance to me was growing weaker. His connection to the forest was too strong. If they have managed to do it...I dread to think..."

Quen's face turned from a smile to a boiling fury.

"If they have turned him back," Quen shuddered, "with that extra dose you gave him, his skin might be too strong to receive any more dog bites. All you have done is empowered one of our enemies, one of the forest's Guardians!"

Fenshin knew what was about to happen.

"I feel that your use, to me, has expired," Quen said. "Goodbye, Fenshin." Quen raised his sword.

"Goodbye, sir," Fenshin said.

Plan

*While plans can be useful, remain open
to the spontaneity of the present moment.*

Chapter 25 - The Garganfans

After Martin and his mother had arrived at their area of the forest, Martin felt the Earthcoat tighten around his body.

"That's strange," Martin said.

"What?" his mother, Amanda, said.

"The coat flinched just then. It made me think of death, as if something had died, or nearly did."

"Everything is living and dying," his mother said, looking around the forest, almost as if she was in a slightly different world.

"No, something worse than that," Martin said. "It felt as if someone was about to be killed by someone else."

The two stood together as they saw one large lorry ahead of them at the road beyond the forest. This one was grey, and it was full of prisoners that had been bitten by the dogs and injected with another powerful serum.

The Garganfan had not yet arrived.

"Where is he?" Martin said, looking around. "He told me to use my coat to transport me and you through the tree roots, didn't he? He should be here by now."

"Don't worry," Amanda said, "he will come."

Martin looked at his mother.

"You shouldn't have to fight," Martin said to her. "I don't want you to."

Amanda looked at Martin.

"I can take care of myself, Martin," she said. "There are powers I developed as a child that you don't realise I have."

"Like what?"

"You'll see. My specialty was always blending and communicating with plant life. As long as I don't let fear get the better of me, as I did with that witch all those years ago, then my powers can still flow through me easily."

"I feel fear," Martin said.

"And it's okay," Amanda said, "I'm sure you've been told that before. Fear is okay. If you embrace it, it can fuel you instead of strangling you into freezing up, like it did with me."

Martin heard movement above them. It looked as if the branches were moving. Then he heard gentle footsteps behind them.

"Sorry we are late. There were more to gather," the Garganfan said. He looked strong and regal. Martin thought that a crown would have suited him well at this point.

Martin looked up again.

"There are more?" Martin said. "More Garganfans?"

"Yes. They have been inactive while I have been missing, but Garganfans are always hungry for battle. That's what we are built for."

"There's a large lorry out there on the road," Martin said. "I don't know what's inside."

"The Strategist has told me that their plan was to unleash their prisoners onto us, the prisoners they have managed to turn into powerful slaves of Quen's mind. There will be creatures in that lorry that once lived here."

"How should we handle them?" Martin said, wondering how much force he should use.

"It isn't for you to decide," the Garganfan said. "It's up to that coat you are wearing. Let it work through you."

Martin looked back into the distance, and he saw two large men opening the back of the lorry, and a swarm of dark, ragged-looking creatures began pouring out, as if they had all been stacked up on top of each other, and they began gathering together on the ground, facing the forest, ready to charge.

*

Myasako, Kuyasaki and Takashi were standing, side by side in the woods, where the Strategist had instructed them to stay. Ahead of them was a dark green lorry. They weren't sure what was inside. They didn't really care.

All three of them were silent. Myasako looked at his father.

"Do not entertain thoughts of defeat," Kuyasaki said, sensing where Myasako's mind was going. "Only focus on victory, be in alignment with victory, and hold no resistance against failure. Failure is never an enemy, unless you decide to make it one. Then it will destroy you from the inside."

Myasako wasn't worried about himself, but he was worried about never seeing his father again.

"You must have faith," Kuyasaki said, still sensing the clarity in Myasako's mind beginning to fade. "Faith in the unseen, faith in what is felt but yet to come. I have taught you a lot, you are far from reaching your full potential, and this battle will take you a step further in your training."

Takashi was absolutely silent. It was as if he had become one with the forest.

"You see what Takashi has done. His mind has melded into the intelligence around us and beneath us. You must do the same. Become one with this forest."

The ancient warlord was standing behind the three ninjas.

"Let me protect you, master," Golhara said. "Allow me to go first, I can not hide in these woods like you can. Stealth is not my ally. My ally is this sword, my strength, my power. Allow me to bear the brunt of the attack, I will not fail you."

"You will serve us well," Kuyasaki said, removing 'failure' from the mind of the warlord. "Thank you, Golhara."

The ancient warlord stepped forward, and now his footsteps were heavier than ever before. Myasako felt the ground beginning to tremble, as if it knew what was about to happen in these woods. The ancient warlord walked past the three ninjas, and began to march slowly towards the lorry in the distance.

"Leave it to me," Golhara said, and he kept walking through the trees and beyond them, and he began to sprint towards the dark green lorry in the distance.

*

"Wait, sir!" Fenshin cried just as Quen was about to slash his sword through his throat.

"We are forgetting something," Fenshin said, humbly, realising that his duty had not yet been fulfilled.

"What?" Quen said.

"The other warlords, sir, they are yet to be awoken."

Quen raised his sword to point to the sky and took a deep breath in.

"The other scientists are awaiting my order," Fenshin said, slowly pulling out a small black mobile phone.

Quen had fallen silent. He let the man do his work.

"Yes, now, now is the time," Fenshin said. "Administer the dosages immediately. And then run. We do not know what the effects will be."

Fenshin hung up the phone and stared at his master.

"This better work," Quen said.

"It should do, sir," said Fenshin, trying to buy himself some time. "Of course it's new technology we are working with, to bring anything back from the dead, to regenerate rotting corpses into living beings again...but hopefully this will work."

Fenshin's phone began to ring. Fenshin picked it up.

"Nothing? It should be instantaneous. Nothing at all?" Fenshin shifted his eyes to look at Quen for a second.

"Perhaps, perhaps you are right," Fenshin said over the phone.

"Ah!" Quen yelled. "The timing of this is all wrong, we should be attacking by now!"

"We can fix this, sir," Fenshin grovelled. "We just need a bit more time. I will hurry to the warlords. You should come with me, since you are their descendent."

Quen was beginning to panic.

"Open the door," Quen said to one of his guards, who rushed to the back of the lorry and sent the contractable door flying up into the top, and piles of dogs began to fall out of the lorry, and gather together, ready to attack the forest.

"Hurry up," Quen said to Fenshin. "Take me to the warlords."

解

決

Solution

Once a problem is identified,
become solution-orientated,
instead of focussing on the problem.

Chapter 26 - The Dark Warlords

As Quen and Fenshin were being driven quickly along the road in their armoured vehicle, they arrived at the lorry containing three motionless warlords, ancestors of Quen who had left instructions for their revival if the medicine was ever developed.

"There they are," Fenshin said.

Fenshin and Quen stepped out of the armoured vehicle, and in the distance they could suddenly see something shining. It was a sword, a huge sword, and holding the sword was Golhara, sprinting out of the woods and running directly towards them.

"Why haven't they woken up!" Quen shouted. "They said to wake them near the forest when there was a mission to complete, didn't they? Why haven't they woken up?"

Soon Golhara was close, and he had spotted Quen.

"Quen! This is no place for war!"

The scientists and extra guards began to back away. Some of the guards from the lorry began to aim and fire their weapons at Golhara, but as soon as they shot him, their bullets bounced off his armour and flew directly back into them.

Fenshin ran and hid behind the lorry.

"I have the empowered sword!" Golhara cried, and as he arrived at Quen he slashed at him. Quen went to block with his own sword, and Golhara's sword cut straight through Quen's. Quen began to back away too. He thought *he* was the empowered one.

"Traitor," Quen said. "You are a descendent of the Great Ferokuma. We are on the same side, we are part of the same clan, and here you are, in defiance of our forefathers' mission!"

"That is not their mission anymore," Golhara replied. "My master realises his wrongdoings. I am here to put them right."

"But my master was different to yours," Quen said. "His desires for power are still strong, and I have brought him and his brothers here to fight for what they want."

Golhara turned around, and out of the lorry began to clamber three other warlords, dark warlords with weapons at their waists – swords and maces and shields that looked as if they had fought in hundreds of battles.

Golhara recognised them all.

"You can not take on all four of us," Quen said, realising his broken sword could be used as an effective stabbing tool.

"Reconsider this," Golhara said, feeling himself become surrounded by other warlords. "Master Ferokuma has sent me here to defend what's right."

"He is misguided," one of the awakened dark warlords said. "His love for the ether and his distaste for the material realm has made him see things differently. He sees things the wrong way, as if there isn't more that our family could take and rule in this realm. He was always the outcast amongst us. We might be brothers, but we always knew he would lose his way."

Golhara stood ready.

"How have you come back to the material realm?" Golhara said.

"We knew it would happen eventually," one of the dark warlords said. All of their armour was dark, and all of their weapons were made from heavy, blackened metal. "Our father prophesised a time during Quen's life, where the medicines would be so great that they would be able to bring back to life the bodies of those that had not decayed too severely. Parts of our flesh still remained, preserved by Quen himself, and now our time has come to join forces along with his dogs, his prisoners, and to expand our empire."

One of the dark warlords swung their mace at Golhara's head. Golhara ducked and swung his empowered sword back. The first dark warlord leaned back to evade, and as the three ninjas watched from the safety of the woods, they knew that they would be needed soon.

*

Myasako, Takashi and Kuyasaki were now sprinting towards Golhara to help him.

Golhara could sense them approaching. His empowered sword was beginning to shine with an even brighter blue colour.

"Stay back, ninjas!" he said. "Do not help me!"

Golhara was battling against Quen and the other three dark warlords, swinging his sword, sometimes missing and sometimes slicing through their armour and into the bodies of the warlords. But as Myasako watched their cuts open up, he saw them quickly seal themselves again, as if they had been filled with potent healing power that refused to see them injured for more than a few seconds.

"Off with their heads!" Golhara cried, and soon he became so empowered by this sword that he was managing to throw the warlords into each other, making them stumble and roll, and one by one, he was cutting off their heads.

Only Quen was left.

"I'm sorry it has come to this," Golhara said, and as he advanced on Quen to strike, the fallen bodies of the dark warlords stood to their feet, grabbed their own heads, and sealed them back into place.

"We cannot be stopped," the warlords said in unison, and as they noticed the ninjas approaching, they began to sprint after them.

"Run, ninjas! Run!" Golhara said, and as he went to strike at Quen, Quen had disappeared round to the other side of the lorry, and was beginning to run, alone, into the woods.

Strike

*Seize opportunities
when they present themselves.*

Chapter 27 - The Battle For The Shinwa Forest

As Quen sprinted towards the forest, he set his intention for every one of his slaves to charge towards the forest and attack, biting anything in their path and primarily going after the Great Dark Wolves Of Japan. Quen didn't know exactly where the wolves were, but he knew that at least one of his groups would find them. If his dogs didn't find them, then the prisoners would, and if the prisoners didn't find the wolves, then the revived warlords were sure to. As he sprinted towards the forest, the apes and the Guardian sitting up in the trees saw the dogs begin to surge towards the forest as one unit.

But now they were ready, the Strategist had briefed the Guardian on what the plan was, and now all the apes were spread across the trees, ready and waiting to drop.

As the dogs flooded towards the forest, some veered off to the left and ran in the direction of Quen. Half of them remained, and continued to sprint directly towards the apes.

As each dog entered the woods, an ape would land on it, then another. They were teaming up, at least two apes to every dog, and as one ape clung to the dog and covered its eyes, the other would carefully but strongly wrap its entire body around the snout of each dog, so they couldn't open and close their mouths anymore.

As the dogs began to run into trees, run into each other and jump and spin and shake to try to get the apes off their backs and snouts, more apes would jump onto the dogs and smother their nostrils so that they couldn't breathe. Gradually and slowly, the dogs began to run out of air, and they would slow to a halt, before keeling over.

But their hearts would not stop beating.

The Guardian had been watching all of this happen, and had seen far off to the left was Quen, running into the woods alongside more wolves.

"I'm going after him," the Guardian said.

"Good luck!" the Strategist shouted from above him, and as the Guardian dropped down to the forest floor and began to run through the woods, he left all the apes behind him, clinging to the dogs.

*

As the Guardian ran through the woods, he could feel all of the extra power that had come to him through the injections he had received at Quen's compound. He was just as loyal and at one with the forest as ever, but now he had extra energy that he had never felt before. He wasn't sure how long it would last, but he could run so fast that soon he was ambushing the dogs that were alongside Quen. There were so many of them that he was surrounded by them, but their bites weren't piercing his skin. Quen was holding a broken blade, and he was beginning to back away in terror.

The Guardian was tearing the dogs apart. He was tearing their limbs off and throwing the limbs far away into the forest, but as he tore and shredded and threw the dogs, he saw their limbs grow back. They regrew legs, they regrew necks and heads, and Quen began to smile.

"Good luck getting through all of them!" Quen said, as the Guardian was fighting his way through slashing teeth and deafening barks, and as the Guardian continued to fight, he saw a group of five apes jump onto Quen and catch him by surprise. They quickly isolated his arm, and the huge gorilla that had been carrying the Strategist managed to rip the sword out of Quen's hand.

"No!" Quen yelled, and as he yelled, the dogs turned to him, and they began to charge towards the apes.

The apes saw them coming and they swung up into the trees, the gorilla still had Quen's sword, and as the dogs ran towards Quen, the Guardian ran towards him too.

"Finally I can get my hands on you!" the Guardian shouted, and as Quen realised the terrible mistake he had made by ever giving the Guardian any extra drugs, the Guardian smashed his fist into Quen's face so hard that Quen flew backwards and hit a tree.

And then the dogs attacked again. They swarmed onto the Guardian, and through the gaps in the ferocious dogs, the Guardian could see the apes quietly swing down and take Quen's limp body up into the trees.

The Guardian felt as if he was losing some energy, as if the power from those drugs was wearing off in the same way that his loyalty to Quen had worn off, and the Guardian jumped out of the leaping and snarling dogs to make his way up to Quen.

He looked down. The dogs could not climb the trees, but they all stopped to sniff the air.

"Kill him! Just kill him!" the Guardian yelled to the apes.

The apes had Quen's body stretched out amongst them. Each had a hand or a leg, and the large dark gorilla was holding Quen's head.

They were trying to pull his body apart, but it wasn't working.

The gorilla was struggling so hard to separate Quen's head from his own body, but it was as if Quen was held to together by some kind of magical force.

The Guardian tried to help, but Quen's body was even tougher than the dogs' bodies. The Guardian didn't know why, then he remembered Fenshin mentioning something about the drugs mixing with Quen's warlord heritage. He looked down at the dogs who continued to sniff, and then seemed to pick up on something.

They turned towards the direction that the Guardian had first come from. They sniffed more and then they sprinted off in the direction of the other apes.

"They can smell the great dark wolves," the Guardian said. "We have to stop them."

*

The Guardian was carrying Quen's body, sprinting through the trees along the ground while the five apes overhead swung through the branches towards the other apes. The dogs were fast, but the Guardian was managing to keep in sight of them. This isn't quite what the Strategist had said would happen.

The Guardian could see in the distance the Strategist was sitting up in a tree. He saw the other dogs running towards the apes that were still trying to suffocate the original twenty.

The Strategist took out a whistle, and he made a sound that forced the Guardian to drop Quen's body and cover his ears.

The dogs did the same. They crashed into the ground and rolled and seemed to writhe around in agony, and when the Strategist stopped whistling, the dogs sensed how close Quen was behind them. Now they were confused. Their master was unconscious, Quen had been knocked out by the Guardian with a mixed desire for himself to be protected, and for the Great Dark Wolves Of Japan to be found, bitten into, and converted into his powerful slaves.

The dogs were staring at Quen, as if they needed an answer, and they began to edge towards the Guardian, knowing they might get torn apart again. The Guardian saw behind them a pack of great dark wolves that seemed to mask everything around them in shadows, wolves so big that he felt a surge of adrenaline rise up within him at the thought of what was about to happen, and riding in front, on top of one of the largest wolves, was a girl who's face had become dark too. It was almost as if she was beginning to rise up off the wolf she was riding, almost as if she was flying.

"No one will take this forest! This forest belongs to the Great Dark Wolves Of Japan!" the girl shouted. Her voice was so powerful that it shook the Guardian's heart, and as the Guardian picked up Quen's body to swing at the vicious dogs, the great dark wolves came crashing in through the dogs and began latching on to the dogs' bodies and shaking the dogs so viciously that the Guardian began to back away.

"You think these are powerful dogs?" the girl said. The Guardian had a sick feeling inside his stomach now. Her voice reminded him of a time when Wolf Witches had become so powerful and vengeful, that their strength had started to become destructive. He saw this girl, Nayla, standing in the center of the chaos of wolves biting the mutant dogs, while a dark force seemed to be flowing out of her body, running through the wolves and making them even more powerful.

Now these huge dogs were starting to look weak and insignificant, and the great dark wolves would tear big chunks out of the dogs' bodies, spitting them out onto the forest floor.

"No power can match that of my ancestors!" Nayla yelled. "The great Wolf Witches!"

Nayla's body rose up off the ground, she became engulfed in a dark red air that seemed to mask her face, and as her face changed shape and changed colour, as if it had been painted by an ancient tribe, the wolves became even more powerful. They were tearing into dogs so ruthlessly that the dogs couldn't repair themselves in time, and as the dogs' bodies turned to discarded pieces of flesh, the Guardian felt Quen begin to wake up.

Nayla felt it instantly. Her glance shot towards Quen, and the Guardian put him down, instinctively.

"Thank you, Guardian," Nayla said, "you have served us so very well. We will take it from here."

The Guardian stepped back. Wolves began to turn towards the dogs that the apes had been holding without air, and they began to work through those dogs until there was barely anything left.

It had almost become quiet where Quen and Nayla stood. Quen got to his feet.

"Where's my sword? My dogs? Wake up!" Quen shouted to the remaining dogs being suffocated by the apes. "Wake up. Take out this witch!"

The dogs seemed to wake and managed to struggle away from the apes, but it was too late. The great dark wolves were soon on them, double-teaming them, tearing them apart from both ends of their bodies.

"This isn't fair," Quen said. "This isn't at all fair. I am unarmed."

Nayla looked up. The gorilla was there above her, holding Quen's sword.

She nodded at the ape and spoke in ape-tongue. The gorilla dropped the sword to the ground in front of Quen.

The Strategist called down from up in the branches.

"Bad idea!" he said. "Do not let him have his own weapon!"

"It's broken," Nayla said.

"Doesn't matter!" the Strategist said. "It's still a blade."

Quen picked up the sword and looked at it.

"You know, I've heard about you," Quen said to Nayla, resigning to the fact that his dogs were now destroyed beyond repair. "A Wolf Witch, in a child's body."

Nayla said nothing. She was going to enjoy this. She still hovered above the ground, and she looked as if she was summoning something from the air around her.

"You won't be able to kill me," Quen said. "It's impossible."

211

Quen raised his broken sword. "Why did you let me have this back?"

"I want to see you fight for your life," Nayla said. "I want you to still think you have a chance of surviving."

"Do you know what will happen in just a few seconds?" Quen said, smiling and seeing his sword start to regain its shape and grow into a strong, shining blade.

Nayla didn't say anything.

"It's already happened," Quen said. "The three warlord brothers I brought with me were awoken on the border of this forest. If just one of them could enter into the woods, he could make the ancient call to resurrect all of the fallen warlords for one final mission."

Nayla began to rise up into the air with fury, and her hands began to fill with darkened silver light.

"And now it is done," Quen said, and as he charged towards Nayla with his sword raised by his side, a hundred warlords sprang through the trees, and they all thrust their blades towards her body.

*

Minutes before, Kuyasaki, Myasako, Takashi and the ancient warlord Golhara had been fighting the other three dark warlords as Quen had managed to escape into the forest.

"We have a mission to complete," one of the dark warlords said. "Do you remember the call?"

"Yes," the other two said, advancing on the ninjas and slashing their weapons at them. They were at least three times the size of Kuyasaki, and the ninjas were rolling around them, trying to pierce through armour that could not even be pierced by bears in wars hundreds of years ago.

"No!" Golhara cried, "No, you will not evoke the call of the fallen warlords. That is only to be used in dire emergencies, for the one time where every fallen warlord is needed to help."

"Yes!" one of the dark warlords cried, "and only one of us must get amongst the trees to do it!"

Golhara could see flashes of light in the corner of his eye, where Martin, Garganfans and Amanda were fighting against a hoard of corrupted prisoners in the forest.

"No! That call only evokes the darkest part of the mind, it is a call of war, not of peace!" Golhara yelled.

He was battling with one of the dark warlords, kicking him to the ground, and then slicing off a leg.

The dark warlord cried out in agony.

"You are a traitor!" the fallen warlord cried.

As Golhara went to finish him, another warlord grabbed Golhara from behind and tried to tackle him to the ground. Golhara dropped, rolled and kicked the fallen warlord away so that he went flying back towards the lorry he had emerged from.

Only one dark warlord was left. As it fought with the three ninjas who were managing to evade all attacks, Golhara crashed into the last dark warlord's body, knocking him to the ground, and then thrusting his sword down into the heart of the dark warlord.

"That was a mistake!" the final warlord winced. "Even the empowered sword is no match for our hearts. We are the Genshonan brothers, you know that! We were the first ones to wield a sword of such power when we found our freedom from foreign invaders. That power is always loyal to us. It had simply lost its way!"

"Oh, no," Golhara said. He could feel a darkness beginning to flow up from the dark warlord's heart and into the sword. "It will infect me. It will infect me if I hold on."

"Then let go!" Kuyasaki yelled.

As the darkness travelled up the blade of the sword from the heart of the fallen dark warlord, the warlord that had been kicked towards the lorry began sprinting back towards the forest.

"I can't take it out!" Golhara cried, trying to pull the sword out of the fallen warlord's body.

"Let it go!" Kuyasaki said again. He took out a dart and threw it towards the advancing warlord's eye. The warlord ducked and continued to charge.

"Yes!" the warlord with the sword in his heart cried. "It is time for you to join us, Golhara!"

"Let it go!" Kuyasaki cried, and as Golhara let go of the sword, the running warlord grabbed the handle, removed the sword, jumped cleanly over the ninjas with a height that seemed to be empowered by the now blackened blade, and he sprinted into the trees.

"Now we are in trouble," Golhara said.

Trouble

Free your mind from unnecessary trouble.

Chapter 28 - Martin And The King

Martin saw them charging. It looked like hundreds of creatures, all looking ragged and starved, creatures he had never seen alongside human beings that looked hungry for something, and they were all running straight towards him, his mother and the team of Garganfans that were now hiding up in the trees.

Amanda ran off to the side, in between trees, and Martin watched her body turn into a huge plant with strong vines resting at its side.

"Remember," the Garganfan said as he stood beside Martin, "let the coat work through you. Don't try to control it."

"Okay," Martin said. He found himself beginning to run, straight towards the gang of prisoners. He could see they were salivating, taken over by Quen's drugs that made them just want to find great dark wolves and bite into anything that got in their way.

Martin ran towards the edge of the forest, and he raised his hands.

"Do not enter!" Martin cried out, and as he threw his hands down into the Earth, it was as if the prisoners were running across a minefield. They were thrown up into the air in groups, and as they tumbled back to the ground they managed to land on their feet and keep running.

"Stop!" Martin yelled, and he threw his hands towards them as a shield of bright white light flew out from his hands, as if it was being fed through him by the coat around his body.

The prisoners all stopped. They couldn't penetrate the wall of light.

The light began to circle and engulf the prisoners. They began to back away and try to run around it.

Martin started to struggle. He didn't fully trust the power of the coat.

"More, it's not enough!" Martin said to the coat as he watched the prisoners begin to back away and run around the wall of light.

The more he noticed that there wasn't enough power, the more the light seemed to fade.

"No, that's not enough!" Martin said, and as he said it again, the light flowing out from his hands faded enough so that the prisoners could run straight through it.

They were running straight towards him.

Now Martin trusted the coat even less, not realising that his mindset had been the thing that had been choking off the power.

He began to back away. There were far too many of them for him to handle, and as he ran backwards, the prisoners all leapt into the barrier of the forest, and began to look for anything they could bite into.

As Martin ran backwards, he saw the Garganfan run past him and head directly towards the prisoners.

The Garganfan didn't say anything. He jumped and swung his staff of roots so fast that a wave of prisoners were knocked back from him.

"The King Of The Trees! The King Of The Trees!" the other Garganfans started to chant, and as if they were one organism, they all dropped down from the trees and began to fight and knock down all the prisoners that managed to reach them. Martin watched his friend, the King Of The Trees, influencing everything around him. Branches from trees were whipping down and knocking more prisoners to the ground. The other Garganfans would pick up the prisoners and throw them out of the forest before they managed to revive themselves.

Martin saw his mother, now standing as a silent plant, ambushing any prisoner that ran past her towards Martin. The vines of the plant would snatch at every prisoner's foot and fling them away out of the woods.

She was acting as Martin's protector, and Martin was watching the entire battle unfold for a moment.

The King Of The Trees was fighting so smoothly and ferociously, it was as if Martin wasn't even needed.

But then Martin heard a call. It sounded like an ancient war cry that flooded throughout the forest. Nothing else seemed to hear it. Perhaps Martin could hear it since he was wearing the Earthcoat, and as soon as the cry ended, Martin felt a presence emerge behind him.

He turned around and saw bodies rising up from the Earth.

They were old, armoured warlords that had fallen many hundreds of years ago. They all stood to their feet, with swords in their hands, and they spotted Martin looking at them.

The few warlords turned into tens, and then tens seemed to turn into hundreds as Martin looked further and further back into the forest.

One of the warlords pointed at him.

"His coat must be removed," the warlord said, and they all began to charge at Martin, swords brandished. Martin suddenly felt such fear flood through him that he couldn't access any power at all.

He couldn't feel his connection with the Earth, he could barely feel the power of the coat around his body. He felt isolated, all of a sudden weak and overcome by the fear of what was about to happen next.

And as Martin raised his hands to fight, knowing that all of his deeper powers had somehow been cut off, the Garganfan jumped over Martin's body, still with his staff of roots in his hand, and he began to single-handedly take on the battalion of warlords, jumping, swinging, kicking and punching any warlord that dared to come near him.

"You are thinking too physically!" the Garganfan said. All the warlords had turned towards him as the main threat. His staff seemed to have the power to knock warlords dead.

"Surrender your physicality to this forest!" the Garganfan cried at Martin.

Martin didn't want to. Surrendering meant death, surrendering meant he would lose his separateness, it felt like he was losing everything about himself that he had been developing over the years, everything that his mum wanted him to be.

The warlords were flooding towards the Garganfan. His courage in battle gave Martin a surge of inspiration. He wanted to be so at one with the forest, so powerful that no one would ever be able to do anything that wasn't right.

He had a feeling rise up in him. It was a feeling of formlessness.

"I'm not helping as I am," Martin said. "So perhaps I should just let the forest do what it wants with me."

He found himself kneeling, putting his head on the forest floor, and it felt as if two great hands were picking him up and standing him to his feet.

He looked around himself. No one was there to have picked him up. The Garganfans behind him were battling with the prisoners, the King Of The Trees was battling the warlords, and now Martin wasn't afraid.

"Use me," Martin said to the forest, and he felt an enormous surge of energy flood through his body, coming up from the Earth and flowing through the coat, and he ran so quickly at the warlords that they all stopped and took a little step back as they saw Martin coming.

Martin flew into them. He was grabbing and throwing and kicking, but he didn't feel any impact with anything. Yet, the warlords were all being knocked back and away, falling into trees or hitting their armoured heads on the ground and not moving after the impact.

"That's it!" the Garganfan said. "It's not about you anymore!"

Martin kept the channel open. He let the forest have its way with him, and soon the warlords were all being knocked back, falling down, and some were even beginning to run away.

"None shall escape," the Garganfan said, and as he went to chase down the few that were remaining, running away from them, Martin turned and saw that a gang of prisoners had made it to his mother, still in the form of a plant, and the prisoners were starting to tear the plant apart.

Martin rose up into the air, and something shot his body towards the prisoners. He raised his arms out to the side of his body and as he saw more prisoners beginning to make their way through the fighting Garganfans and bite and tear into the plant that was his mother, Martin felt a bright green light shoot out of his arms and slice through every prisoner that remained in the woods.

Everything stopped. The Garganfans stopped fighting. None of them seemed to have been bitten, but the plant that Martin's mother had morphed into was now cut in half, drooping, and the remaining half that was in the ground changed shape, until it was her human body, lying on the floor.

Martin saw his mother's face. It was cut. She didn't have any energy left.

"I'm sorry, Martin," she said. "They got me. They bit into me. Something's changing..."

"No. No, Mum," Martin said. He saw her body start to change shape. It was almost becoming pinker.

"I felt them infect me," she said. "I felt it. I let you down. You have to kill me! I'm turning into one of them!"

"Mum. You are well. You are healed."

As Martin said those words, he felt the most benevolent force flow out through his hands and reach into his mother's cuts and bruises. He saw them begin to heal themselves.

"You are well, Mum, you are well."

The coat was doing something that Martin had never experienced. It was taking back every bad thing that had ever happened to his mother, as if it had never happened at all.

Her eyes were closed, but her cuts were healing, and her breathing started to become deeper and more relaxed.

"Thank you," she said. "Thank you, Martin. You don't need me anymore. I think I'm going to go now."

Martin didn't expect her to say that. He wanted his mum to be well.

"No, Mum," he said, feeling the healing energy start to become choked off as soon as he said 'no'.

"You have to let me go," she said. "I'm far more powerful if I merge with these trees. I can become a Light Being, I can recruit the others to stop what is happening. This is happening elsewhere, Martin, more warlords are here, Nayla is in trouble."

Martin felt so much struggle beginning to arise from within him.

"I want you to be well, Mum," he said. "I want you to be happy. But I don't want you to..."

"Let me," she said. "I'm not leaving you. I promise."

Martin focussed on what he wanted for his mum. He wanted her to be at peace, free from pain, free from struggle and where she wanted to be.

Martin kissed her on the cheek.

"Now go and help the others," she said. "I will be with you."

Amanda took one more deep breath in, and then she let one last breath out. She didn't breathe in again.

Martin couldn't believe it. He expected her to say something else. The Garganfans were crowded around him, and then the King Of The Trees ran up to them.

"There are others we must help. I have heard the bears calling," the King Of The Trees said. "Let's go."

The Garganfans all followed the King Of The Trees as he ran off into the woods. Martin didn't move.

"Martin, we need you!" the King Of The Trees called, and as Martin let go of all the resistance he had, he started to cry, and the coat took over his whole body, and covered him in darkness.

悲嘆

Grief

Grief is a natural part of life,
and need not be fought against.

Chapter 29 - The Resurrection

As soon as the dark warlord had escaped from Myasako, Takashi, Kuyasaki and Golhara, he had made it into the forest and began to make his ancient call.

"Heera Mondoo Klesna Bakna!"

The sound echoed through the trees and he knew it had been received by every fallen warlord that lay resting in the forest. But before he saw any warlords rise, he saw two savage creatures running towards him.

It was two large brown bears, and before he could even ready himself with his powerful sword, they were on him, knocking him to the ground and starting to tear his helmet away from his head.

He dropped his sword by accident. He was trying to reach for it as one of the bears clamped its jaws around his arm and started trying to tear it out of the socket.

The sword seemed to be lying dormant. It was as if it wasn't sure who to serve. This dark warlord, one of the Genshonan brothers, had helped give rise to the empowered sword's life, to win their own freedom, but now they wanted the sword's power to enslave. The power that the warlord could see emanating out of the sword started to fade away.

"No!" the dark warlord said. "No I need you!" The bears were ripping and tearing and the warlord could feel his arm start to come away from the socket of his shoulder.

The other bear was managing to remove his helmet.

"Help me!" the warlord cried, and as his helmet was removed, and he could see more clearly than ever before, he saw a group of dark warlords emerging out of the trees and attacking the bears.

"Yes!" the warlord cried out. "Yes!"

He was still on the floor, and a battle ensued above him.

The bears were angry and ferocious, and the warlords had not moved their bodies for hundreds of years.

The bears were impenetrable to any slash of sword, and the bears were managing to out-wrestle and out-bite all of the warlords that came towards them.

Then the dark warlords began to fall.

Darts and ninja stars were being thrown into their eyes through the small gaps in their helmets, and a small figure of a boy dressed in black seemed to be skipping between all of the warlords and striking at their ankles with nunchuks and a dagger.

Another ninja was falling from the trees, a thin and ferocious-looking ninja who was driving his sword directly down into the collarbones of the ancient warlords, through very thin gaps in their armour.

And then Golhara leapt in amongst the crowd, picked up the sword from the ground, and the light and power in his sword that he once had began to re-emerge.

"No!" the dark warlord cried, still on the floor, starting to cower away. "No! The power is changing allegiance!"

"And now we are in the forest, where the power originated!" Golhara yelled. Every slash of his sword knocked back ten incoming warlords, and the more flooded towards him, the more he was able to knock back.

"Nothing can beat this sword, the empowered sword in the hands of good!" Golhara cried, and he kept fighting, knocking back warlords with such strength that the pure light from the sword seemed to make their bodies freeze and become incapacitated. Soon the dark warlords were dwindling in numbers, and the ninja that had been on top of the warlords, Takashi, noticed the first dark warlord on the ground, trying to stand to his feet.

The dark warlord felt the ninja land on his back, and drive a blade deep through his neck, down into his body, and he felt the blade touch his heart.

"Goodbye," Takashi said. "For good."

Justice

While justice can be satisfying,
the need for it can destroy one's peace of mind.

Chapter 30 - The Power

As a huge group of warlords along with Quen charged at Nayla with raised swords, the wolves leapt into action to intercept them. They were hugely outnumbered. All of the hundreds of warlords that had fallen over time in the forest had been summoned mostly towards Nayla and the wolves, where Quen's targets were located, and as the wolves dived in front of Nayla to protect their Queen, as they grabbed hold of warlords in their teeth to tear them apart, other warlords were beginning to stick their blades into the bodies of wolves.

Two wolves jumped on Quen and started trying to rip his limbs off his body, but still, even without armour, he seemed impenetrable.

The Guardian charged towards the warlords and tried to help the wolves. He was ducking and punching and grabbing at the warlords' ankles so that the wolves could finish them off, but the number of warlords was so great that the Guardian was starting to become overwhelmed, and he couldn't stop the occasional warlord from seeping through and thrusting a blade into a wolf.

Nayla watched what was happening and she lost control of her mind.

Quen saw her through the wolves as he tried to fight them off with his sword. Nayla rose up so high that she almost disappeared amongst the canopy of trees, and her entire body became shrouded in darkness.

"No!" she yelled out, and a force of a thousand Wolf Witches from the beginning of time flowed through her body and smashed down into the ground, knocking down every warlord that there was in the forest.

The warlords didn't move. Quen wasn't moving, either.

The three ninjas and Golhara arrived. Hinzen had been told to hide somewhere high up in the trees. The Ferahawk birds that the Strategist had told to wait were now swooping in and trying to remove the warlords' helmets as they began to wake up again.

"Why won't they die?" Nayla said, as the apes began to move towards them too.

The Garganfan, now seen by everyone as the King Of The Trees, along with his team of Garganfans, appeared soon after. Martin found himself still covered in the Earthcoat, but now he was kneeling beside the Garganfan, looking up to see what was going on.

"You cannot defeat them with darkness," the Garganfan said. "They can only be defeated with light."

"Nonsense!" Nayla said, and again, just as the Ferahawk birds, the Guardian and the apes managed to move out of the way, clouds of black smoke flew out of Nayla's hands and went deep into the warlords' bodies.

They began to rise up.

"That's too much darkness," the Garganfan said. "You are empowering them. The Wolf Witches are capable of light, but your anger is attracting the darkness."

"What's wrong with anger!" Nayla said, throwing more and more darkness onto the warlords and Quen, who were standing to their feet even faster.

"Nothing," the Garganfan said, "unless it becomes blinding. Then it can make you do things you regret."

"Let me deal with this!" Nayla said. She could feel so much power, but it was almost as if she was beginning to fight against herself, almost as if she was becoming a tool of Quen's intentions.

"She cannot escape her own anger," Quen said, smiling up at Nayla. "The more she fights her anger, the more it will help us from here on in."

"Shut up!" Nayla said. She was overwhelmed with fury. All she wanted was death, for Quen to die, for the warlords to die, and the more she tried to fight against herself, to stop her anger from empowering the warlords, the angrier she became.

"You have to stop fighting against yourself!" Martin called up at Nayla.

Quen turned towards him.

"You need to use the power of the forest, not just the past pain of other people!" Martin said. He could see that every dark part of the Wolf Witches' history was now seeking expression, almost wanting to create more of itself.

"Quiet, boy!" Quen said, and he began to run towards Martin.

Martin snapped his fingers, and Quen froze in mid-air.

"What are you doing?" Quen said. "Let me go."

Martin saw the Ferahawk birds flying in again to try to tear at the warlord's eyes. There were great dark wolves on the ground, bleeding, with more warlords trying to finish them off. In the distance Martin could see all of the other creatures the Strategist had gathered, all fighting against hundreds of warlords further in the woods that were trying to make their way towards the wolves.

"Stop," Martin said. "This all has to stop."

He snapped his fingers again, and everything around him went into suspension.

The only thing still moving was the Garganfan.

"It's your mother," the Garganfan said. "She is helping you. Her power combined with that coat, combined with the union you are now developing with the forest. You have unbelievable amounts of power."

"Really?" Martin said. "Well where is Mum?"

Martin was looking around.

"You can't see her. But you can feel her presence," the Garganfan said.

The Garganfan was right. Martin could feel his mother all around him, stretching throughout the forest and working with him.

In the distance Martin saw two other beings, two Light Beings – Hirozama, Kuyasaki's old master, and the Mountain Man, with a bright shining eagle on his shoulder.

"More Light Beings," Martin said.

As they approached, the Mountain Man was smiling. Hirozama bowed at the Garganfan, who bowed back.

"The King Of The Trees," Hirozoma said. "We heard you had returned."

"Great to see you again," the Mountain Man said. He turned to Martin. "We had to come and see you too, young man. A new Earthman, with an Earthcoat as well!"

Both Hirozama and the Mountain Man dropped to one knee and bowed their heads. So did the Garganfan.

"You have the utmost power in these forests," the Garganfan said. "In this moment, with the clarity and power flowing through you, you can shape things to be how you want them."

"I want Quen to turn into a tree," Martin said. "A good tree who obeys the King Of The Trees."

Quen's body started to shift very slowly. It started to turn brown and woody.

"I want the wolves to go back to full health," Martin said. Very slowly, while everything around them was still frozen, the wolves' wounds began to heal.

"I want these dark warlords to rest in peace," Martin said, "to leave this place and go back into the Earth."

Warlords in Martin's vision slowly began to turn into dust.

"And I want Nayla to be freed from the pain of her ancestors," Martin said. "Free to use her powers for healing and harmony in these woods."

Nayla began to slowly lighten up as she stood suspended in the air above the wolves.

"And finally," Martin said, "I want all of those fallen prisoners that were poisoned and drugged by Quen to find their happiest place, whether it is in these woods, back with their families, or even in the formless realm. I want everything to be well."

Martin instinctively snapped his fingers again, and what he wanted to happen, happened. The warlords crumbled, the great dark wolves stood to their feet, Quen turned into a tree, and Nayla came back down to the ground, shining with bright light.

Kuyasaki, Takashi and Myasako looked around, not realising what had happened. Kuyasaki saw his master, Hirozama, and bowed.

"Thank you for coming, master," Kuyasaki said.

Hirozama bowed back.

Myasako and Takashi bowed too, also seeing the Mountain Man was standing there, waving at them. Nayla was tending to the wolves, now on the ground, astonished that they were all well and the warlords were disappearing around them.

Martin felt the coat around his body begin to shrivel up and fall away.

"It's done. It's done with you!" a voice said from the trees. It was Jericho, the Coatmaker's grandson, and he clambered down a tree and brushed Martin off at the shoulders.

"It doesn't stay with you forever," Jericho said. "Only as long as it wants. You can still develop that kind of power, but it wants you to develop it from the inside, so no one can take it away from you."

Martin looked around. He wished his mother was there.

"She is here," the Garganfan said. "Remember that. You can always feel her presence if you wish to tune into it."

Martin's eyes started to flood with tears.

"She's coming back though, isn't she?"

The Garganfan stood motionless.

"She hasn't gone anywhere," he said.

Immortality

*The immortal realm exists
throughout the present moment.*

Chapter 31 - The Celebration

Martin had never seen a celebration in the forest before. He had never seen wolves dancing. Around a large fire, everyone had gathered – every creature in the forest that had been battling warlords throughout the woods, all of the wolves and their Queen, the Guardian, the three ninjas, the two bears, the Ferahawk birds, the great apes, Golhara, and the team of Garganfans with the King Of The Trees were all together around a fire.

Three of the apes were beating on drums they had made from fallen pieces of wood that Martin had never seen being used as instruments before. The apes would occasionally grunt and howl in time with the beats they were producing, and many of the creatures sitting around the fire couldn't help but move in rhythm.

"I just wanted to see this," Golhara said. "The great celebration. And now it is my time to rest. I am leaving you now, master, to find the perfect place to lay my body down."

Kuyasaki had not sat down. Neither had Takashi. Kuyasaki bowed to the warlord, Golhara bowed back, and then they embraced.

"Thank you," Kuyasaki said. "Thank you for your service, Golhara."

"It has been an honour, master," Golhara said, and as he bowed to Takashi and Myasako, who also bowed back, the ancient warlord turned, walked into the darkness of the forest, and disappeared in the night.

"The forest is usually not safe for young boys," the Garganfan said, sitting next to Martin.

Martin looked at him, remembering a time where he had made the mistake of wandering into the forest at night alone, looking for the ancient protective stone that was now the Garganfan's heart.

"But you are no longer a young boy," the Garganfan smiled. "You are a young Earthman."

Martin looked into the fire, and then into the forest. Beyond the creatures crowded round, dancing and moving and talking and sometimes leaping at the relief of no longer being invaded by any evil intent. Martin was sure that in the distance he could see the figure of his mother, and she was standing next to a man. Martin stood up and waved.

His mother waved back. Martin began to walk around the group of creatures and move towards the couple. They were both shining with a white light, like spirits, and as Martin walked up towards them, the man beside his mother was smiling. He looked big and strong.

"Mum," Martin said. He wanted to hug her.

"Martin, this is my friend that I told you about, from when I was younger. This is Greg," she said.

"Hello, Martin. Tremendous job, mate," Greg said, holding out his hand for Martin to shake. Martin took it. He could feel it as if it was a normal hand. His mother hugged him, just like she used to.

"I don't get it," Martin said. "Are you dead?"

"What do you mean by that?" his mother smiled.

"Are you...are you gone?"

"We are right here," Amanda said. "What people often think about death isn't really true. There's more to it than they think. This was right for me, dear, but I knew I would always be around you, probably more useful than I was before."

Martin looked at the two of them.

"Thanks for your help earlier," Martin said. "The Garganfan was telling me you were helping me."

"Of course," Amanda said. "But you were the one who was ready to receive the help. There's little point in struggling alone, cut off from everything else, is there?"

"No," Martin said. "No." He looked around at the forest. "I don't know what to do now," he said. "I want to stay here, but then there's school, there's Nerris, there's all the normal stuff back home."

"It will be easy," Amanda said. "Don't worry about it. You and Nerris will have a good time living together, and you will do great things in the forest back home. I'm always with you. So is Greg. Now go back to the celebration. And make your way home with the Garganfan when it's time."

"Okay," Martin said. "I love you."

"I love you too, Martin," Amanda said.

*

Everyone slept out in the forest that night. Even without the Earthcoat, Martin was able to summon a giant golden tent of light that kept everyone warm and safe, and when the sun began to rise, he woke up to see Kuyasaki, already standing and waiting for the others.

"Our time has come to leave," Kuyasaki said. "Thank you for coming, Martin, for using your skills, for helping this place."

Martin bowed. "Of course," he said. "Thank you, Kuyasaki, for training me, for getting me started, and for your son, Myasako, thank you again Myasako for saving my mum when you came to stay with her."

Myasako bowed. "My pleasure," he said.

They had all heard what happened to Amanda, and the ninjas seemed united in the understanding that the barriers between life and death were more illusory than people tended to think.

"And we must get you home," the Garganfan said to Martin. "Your work here is done. I will accompany you."

"How will we get back?" Martin said.

"I think you know how," the Garganfan said. "Except this time, you won't need the Earthcoat to do it."

Return

Returning to the source of your thoughts
brings renewed inspiration.

Chapter 32 - The Goodbye

After Martin had said goodbye to everyone and everything else in the forest, after he had been met with hugs from giant apes and bears, gentle pecks on the cheek from Ferahawk birds and pats on the back from a myriad of creatures he had never seen before, Martin closed his eyes, and pictured where he wanted to go.

"Wait," someone said. Nayla was standing in front of him, with her pack of wolves standing behind her.

"We haven't thanked you properly," Nayla said. "For what you did. For how you've helped us."

All the wolves behind Nayla lowered their faces to touch the ground. Nayla stepped closer towards Martin.

"Thank you," she said. She put her arms around him. He put her arms around her, and for a moment, for Martin, it was as if nothing else existed in the forest apart from Nayla.

"Goodbye," Martin said. "And of course, you're welcome. I'm glad I could help."

The two stood in front of each other, Nayla bowed slightly, turned, and led her wolves away, slowly, until Martin couldn't see them anymore.

"It's time," the Garganfan said, standing at Martin's side.

"Okay," Martin said. "By the power of the Earth, I am back in my home forest. By the power of the Earth, I am back at home." Martin took the Garganfan's hand, and they were both sucked down into the power of the Earth, shot through the hidden communication networks of trees that expanded even beyond the seas, where no physical roots could be found, and within a matter of seconds their bodies re-emerged into Martin's forest at home.

"That was even easier," Martin said. "That was even quicker, wasn't it?"

"Your powers are still expanding," the Garganfan said. "You can sense that everything is connected. I look forward to seeing more from you."

"Thank you, for everything," Martin said. He put his thickening arms around the Garganfan and held him tight.

"And thank you, Martin," the Garganfan said, "for showing me my rightful place, as King Of The Trees."

"I'm going back to see Nerris," Martin said. "See you again soon."

"See you," the Garganfan said, and as Martin walked away, he turned back, and saw the Garganfan sit, place his staff of roots by his side, and it was as if every tree in the forest turned toward him slightly, and bowed.

*

When Martin got to Nerris's house, he knocked on the door.

He heard Nerris stop what she was doing and come running up the stairs from the basement. She opened the door.

"Martin! Martin look at you. You look even bigger! Completely different! What's been happening? Where's your mum?"

She beckoned him in and smacked him on the back with encouragement.

"I've got a lot to tell you, Nerris," Martin said. "Let's sit down."

Goodbye

While surrounded by those you love,
be grateful for their presence.

Chapter 33 - The Farewell

After Kuyasaki, Myasako and Takashi had bid farewell to everyone in the forest, including Nayla and her wolves, they promised they would come back to see her in two weeks.

"Bring my mum," Nayla said, gently stroking the body of a wolf. "I don't want to cut myself off from her, or from you, but I know that my true home is here."

"We will see you again, in two weeks," Kuyasaki said, bowing.

As the ninjas made their way out of the forest, Myasako had a strange feeling of emptiness, as if there was no longer anything to accomplish. Everything had been done.

"What now?" Myasako said, feeling slightly unsettled that there was no longer anything left to conquer.

"Now we return to peace," Kuyasaki said. "We return to our normal way of life. We appreciate the peace we have where we live, and we continue to develop our skills."

Takashi wasn't saying anything. Myasako was amazed that all of them seemed to have emerged from yesterday's battle unscathed. Takashi had a scratch on his neck from being clawed at by a dark warlord's hand, but that was it.

"Thank you for teaching me so well, Father," Myasako said. "It's because of you that I could help yesterday."

"You are the one who has done the training," Kuyasaki said. "Don't forget to credit yourself."

As the three ninjas continued to walk out of the forest, they saw something moving in the distance.

"What's that?" Myasako said. Takashi drew his sword.

"Easy, Takashi," Kuyasaki said. "It's a young boy and a very unusual creature. I don't know what that is."

As they approached the two small figures in the distance, the young boy seemed to notice them.

"Help! Please! My friend, he's hurt."

Kuyasaki began to trot up to the pair, with a hand resting on a dagger at his waist.

In front of them was a boy, Myasako's age, and at his feet was a brown creature with a wide head and large eyes, and it was bleeding from its body.

"Normally he can re-heal, but for some reason it's not working!" the boy said.

"Takashi," Kuyasaki said. "Ginzen Leaves, quickly. There should be some around here. Myasako, help Takashi find some Ginzen Leaves. You know what they look like."

Myasako and Takashi ran off together to search, and Kuyasaki stayed with the pair.

"I'm Wallace," the boy said. "This is Fred."

"Where have you come from?" Kuyasaki said.

"We were travelling," Wallace said, "through the underground portals, but we couldn't make it back home to England. Fred is too hurt."

The strange-looking creature called Fred had eyes that were struggling to stay open.

Soon Takashi arrived back with a handful of Ginzen Leaves. Myasako arrived soon after.

Kuyasaki grabbed some from Takashi.

"Chew. Chew!" Kuyasaki said to all of them. The taste was so bitter that Myasako nearly spat it out. He remembered the leaves from when he had been slashed by a Korokoshin Monster.

"Now apply the paste," Kuyasaki said to the two ninjas, as he also finished chewing. The three ninjas spat out the paste of leaves and patted it down into the bleeding area of Fred's body.

Fred screamed so loudly that Myasako covered his ears.

Wallace looked terrified, stumbled back and covered his ears too.

After a few seconds the screaming subsided, and Fred stood to his feet.

"We are indebted to you," Fred said, bowing at the ninjas. "Your service will not go unrewarded. We thank you. But we cannot stay. We must go."

Fred took Wallace's hand.

"Thank you! Thank you so much," Wallace said. "You've helped the planet more than you realise."

Fred simply nodded his head, closed his eyes, and the two suddenly vanished.

The forest was quiet again.

"How odd," Kuyasaki said. "I've never seen or heard of a creature like that before. It looked almost other-worldly."

"I wonder what they've been up to," Myasako said.

"Indeed," Kuyasaki said. "Now let's go home, there's something I want to show you back at the dojo. You are ready for it now. If I'd shown you it before, you might not have taken it seriously."

"What is it?" Myasako said.

"It's a book about your heritage, our ancestors. Tales of ninjas over the course of time who have managed to develop or were born with fantastic powers during their lifetimes. Powers that most would believe to be pure fantasy."

"Okay," Myasako said, looking forward to keeping some kind of adventure alive. "What's the book called?"

"It's called The Ninja Chronicles," Kuyasaki said.

The Ninja Chronicles – Part 1

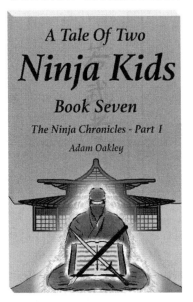

"Fred: The Creature Sent To Save Us All"

- OUT NOW ON AMAZON! -

You have met Fred at the end of "A Tale Of Two Ninja Kids - Book 6", and now you can join his adventures with Wallace as he tries to save the Chatamanga Rainforest from destruction, uncovering a strange new world that Wallace never expected...

10% of profits will be used to plant new trees.

Get the book now on Amazon!

"Mythical Creatures Of The Forest"

- OUT NOW ON AMAZON! -

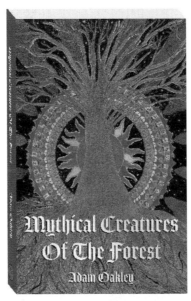

Discover more stories about the Garganfan, the Mountain Man, and learn about when Amanda and Greg first discovered the magic of the forest.

Meet the Dundenbeast, the Shapeshifter, Heelog, the Treekeeper, the Feasting Tree, the Pikaloo, the Healybug and many others...

Join Dr Bernard J. Hoothfellow as he embarks on his mission to discover all the creatures in the forest that no one believes to be real.

Adventure awaits.

Get the book now on Amazon!

"Happiness Is Inside: 25 Inspirational Stories For Greater Peace Of Mind"

- OUT NOW ON AMAZON! -

Inspirational short stories for ages 8 and up...

Meet the boy who could not worry, the man who has become free from labels, the mysterious bear who has wisdom to share, and the frog who has discovered the secret to lasting joy.

These are great stories for parents and children to read together or alone, and each have their own message for a more fulfilling life.

Get the book now on Amazon!

"Henrik The Defender"

- OUT NOW ON AMAZON! -

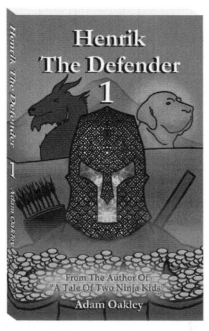

Discover the adventures of the noble warrior Henrik The Defender as he moves into adulthood and his fighting skills are put to the test.

Join Henrik and his loyal Fighting Hound named Boevill as they work together to protect the Kingdom of Argad from an evil force, alongside some of the magical fighting creatures from Henrik's past...

Get the book now on Amazon!

Audiobooks

Audiobooks available on Amazon, Audible, Apple and AdamOakleyBooks.com

Book Reviews

ENJOYING THE SERIES?

PLEASE LEAVE SOME GOOD REVIEWS ON AMAZON TO HELP THE BOOKS REACH YOUNG NINJAS EVERYWHERE!

THANK YOU!

About The Author

Adam is an author from the UK who loves to write all different kinds of books.

He writes books about inner peace, inner power, and loves writing stories that feel like stepping into other realms.

He spends his time writing, doing martial arts, growing organic food and spending time with his family.

He hopes you loved reading the book, and he is grateful for any young readers or parents who can leave a review on Amazon to help the book reach more people.

He thanks you for your support, and is always available to contact via one of his websites:

www.InnerPeaceNow.com

www.AdamOakleyBooks.com

Made in the USA
Columbia, SC
07 December 2022